Merry Christmas
from Ian + Lynne

W9-BHK-225

EARS OF THE JUNGLE

Other Books by Pierre Boulle

The Bridge Over the River Kwai
Planet of the Apes
Garden On the Moon
Because It is Absurd
My Own River Kwai
The Photographer
Time Out of Mind
The Executioner
A Noble Profession
S.O.P.H.I.A.
The Other Side of the Coin
The Test
Face of a Hero
Not the Glory

EARS
OF THE
JUNGLE

PIERRE BOULLE

Translated by Michael Dobry and Lynda Cole

CASSELL · LONDON

CASSELL & COMPANY LTD
35 Red Lion Square, London WC1R 4SG
Sydney, Auckland, Toronto,
Johannesburg

Originally published as *Les Oreilles de Jungle*
Copyright © 1972 by Flammarion
Translation copyright © 1972 by Vanguard Press, Inc.

First published in Great Britain 1974

ISBN 0 304 29352 0

Printed in Great Britain by
Northumberland Press Limited
Gateshead
F 274

Contents

1 The Jarai, *1*

2 Crickets, *47*

3 Napalm, *73*

4 The Ho Chi Minh Way, *91*

5 Wreath of Orchids, *143*

I

THE JARAI

I

There were no sirens to give the alarm. The copper gong, used without much conviction in imitation of the plains people since the bombings had begun, remained silent. All Jarai hill tribesmen possessed sharp enough hearing to detect the sound of aircraft from afar, and besides they were not the target. In the new village built on a high peak of the Annamite chain in an attempt to escape both the morbid persecutions of Diem and the fire stones dropped by the flying men, they were relatively secure. The obscure and mysterious network of the Ho Chi Minh Trail passed some distance to the west, and the fire stones tended to strike the passes, not the peaks. Nevertheless, a light convoy occasionally took the trails of the high country, and the American pilots would now and again drop bombs in the vicinity of their eagle's nest, perhaps by accident, perhaps discharging the forgotten remnants of a load before returning to the fold, or maybe even on the basis of information, whether true or false. Accordingly, with each new moon the Jarai never failed to sacrifice a cock to *yang*[*] Driang, the red, the malevolent spirit, and to his accomplice *yang* Dri, who killed for the pleasure of killing.

The sacrifice was performed according to an ancient ritual, and, as the cock was completely drained of blood, Mok, the old chief of the village, recited a prayer that began: 'I call now the spirit Driang, the spirit Dri, the evil spirits, the spirits of destruction.'[†]

The Jarai only addressed prayers to the evil spirits; the

[*] The Jarai word for spirit.
[†] *Jarai Prayers* (P. B. Lafont, Ecole française d'Extrême-Orient).

others, the good spirits, had no need of supplications or sacrifices: for they were benevolent.

After this ceremony the Jarai felt somewhat relieved. Nevertheless, on the advice of old Ami,* to whom everyone listened, whenever the roar of the flying machines drew near, and especially when the explosions made the neighbouring mountains tremble, they silently sought the fissures in the rocks that had been hollowed out by the wind and rain, which instinct told them were the safest shelters. Old Ami thought it right to seek the favour of the spirits, but that should not prevent man from taking certain precautions of his own. Whether by the grace of the placated *yang* Driang or as a result of Ami's prudent wisdom, none of the hill tribesmen had been hurt since their emigration to the mountaintop.

That is what they had done this particular night, as the centre of the raid seemed only a few hours' march away and two missiles had landed on the hills close by. The families stayed in the shelters for the duration of the holocaust, perhaps twenty minutes, after which the jungle regained its nocturnal serenity and Chief Mok, straightening up, signalled that the alarm was over. Then, following a fairly recent procedure, the hunters of the village gathered round him to deliberate. The women and children formed a wider circle around them and, though taking no part in the discussion, occasionally commented in lowered voices.

'The stones fell in the direction of the setting sun,' Mok began, 'not far from the Plain of a Hundred Thousand Buffalo.... What do you think, Dju?'

Dju was the best hunter in the village and one of the most famous of his tribe. No one knew the jungle, the invisible trails taken by the animals, better than he. No one knew so well how to approach a herd of wild buffalo—favourite prey of the Jarai—without alerting them, coming within range of the finest beast and releasing a deadly arrow, then finishing it off with his spear. He had never been seen coming back from an expedition empty-handed, and the youth of the village

* The Jarai word for mother.

4

always awaited his return in the hope of bounty, delighted to see him appear bent under the weight of a regal trophy. At least, that's what had happened before. Now the war disrupted the habits of the game and interfered severely with the hunter's activity.

'I don't think the stones fell on the Plain of a Hundred Thousand Buffalo,' he said with a shake of his head, having scented the odour of gunpowder now mingling with the mouldy smell of the jungle. 'Lower than the setting sun, and closer to us.'

'How far?'

'Four or five hours at least. I know the way. It's difficult—there are no trails.'

Squatting around Mok, most of the men had lit curve-stemmed pipes, and some of the women in the larger circle did the same. Mok held a flashlight in his hand, an old gift from a French settler. Its batteries were now dead, but he was rarely separated from it, day or night. It had come to be a symbol of his authority.

The bombings, when not dangerously close, were always followed by long deliberations. The villagers, particularly the children, joyously welcomed any incident out of the ordinary that might serve as the pretext for a prolonged night of festivities. Before, these had most often been occasioned by the return of a group of hunters bearing precious booty after a long expedition: a captured elephant, Indian ox horns of remarkable size, enough meat for several days. Then the women, young girls, and children, wide-eyed at the sight of such wonders, would leave their huts, light a fire on the outskirts of the village, and surround the heroes who, as they drank rice wine from a jug, recounted their exploits, providing the subject for low-voiced comments until daybreak. Songs and rounds would punctuate the tales. At sunrise everyone returned fresh and fit to his normal occupation: tilling the fields.

The bombings had come to provide the opportunity for these popular gatherings, except that there were no longer fires. Mok had forbidden them after realizing they attracted the flying men as a torch attracts nocturnal insects. So it was that the entire village now sat in the darkness, listening to the counsels of their chief as they impatiently awaited his conclusions, though quite prepared to remain there all night if necessary.

'Nearer than the Plain of a Hundred Thousand Buffalo?' Mok repeated anxiously. 'In the black hills then? Not a very favourable region.'

'Wretched mountains, in fact,' Dju agreed. 'Even grass doesn't grow there. I once followed a wounded buffalo that had taken refuge there since the tigers and panthers had deserted them just like most of the other animals ... yet among the hills are a few rare valleys that are more hospitable.'

'Do you think it is worth the trouble of going there?'

Dju hesitated and raised his head; his nostrils flared as he again questioned the exhalations of the jungle.

'Dju cannot answer,' he said at last.

'If Dju does not say no, it means there is a chance,' a voice said.

Someone else had come to join in the debate, a very old woman who had approached soundlessly in the darkness. Ami had waited for the alarm to end before coming out of her hut, for although she recommended others to take shelter, she disdained to do so herself. The Jarai never censured this attitude, for everyone knew Ami was invulnerable. The evil spirits bowed down before her and the good protected her. She was as safe squatting on the mat in her hut of straw as under several feet of concrete. In any case, no one dared criticize a sign or even a word of hers. The villagers, and especially Mok, solicited her opinion whenever they had an important decision to make, and the chiefs of the other villages scattered through the mountains often came to consult her. Never issuing an order, she simply expressed her own way of seeing things, one which the Jarai had come to realize was sound.

She walked with a nonchalant though firm step, holding

6

between her lean fingers a pipe lit during the alert. She crossed the circle of women and children, who had spontaneously risen to their feet at the sound of her voice. The hunters, including Mok, also stood up, for Ami rarely emerged from the raised hut in which she lived alone. Her presence was considered an auspicious event. She repeated: 'If Dju cannot say no, it means there is a chance.'

She spoke in a restrained voice that held no suspicion of command, or even of a wish. In the same tone she added: 'Your children have empty bellies and tomorrow is an "odd" day.'*

'Let us go,' decided Mok. 'Ami is right. A five-hour march is not far. We shall be there before dawn.'

A murmur of agreement rippled through the group of hunters and was prolonged in muffled echoes among the women and children. Since the beginning of the alert everyone had hoped for this decision. A breach formed in the large circle, leaving a passage free for the men about to go into the jungle. It closed behind them and the conversations resumed in subdued voices, expressing now anxiety, now doubt, sometimes hope. As for Ami, she had already taken the path back to her solitude and was climbing the rough notches cut in the stout bamboo pole that served as a ladder to the raised platform of her hut.

The men disappeared into the forest. They walked in single file behind Mok, who carried an old locally manufactured gun on his shoulder and held the useless flashlight in his hand, like a field-marshal's baton. He was preceded by Dju, the best guide for this expedition. Dju also possessed a gun, but it was never taken on hunting trips; it remained in his hut to be used, point-blank if necessary, against any intruder. In the jungle he trusted only his arrows and spear. The others were equipped in the same way; anticipating the possibility of an expedition, they had taken the precaution of collecting their weapons before leaving the huts. The woven

* Generally an auspicious day for the Jarai.

blankets in which they had enveloped themselves for an extended stay in the shelters had been cast off and left in the safekeeping of their wives, and now their only garment was a cord about the loins, from which hung the indispensable machete and various shreds of material, perhaps meant to represent a loincloth. Each wore long ivory earrings and bracelets of metal.

'I wouldn't want us to return empty-handed, like last time,' Mok said anxiously to Dju ahead of him. 'Are you hopeful?'

'As Ami said, it is a matter of luck.'

'Ami always speaks wisely,' the old chief concluded, shaking his head.

2

'Are you going to be finished with that decoding soon?' Madame Ngha asked impatiently.

Van, her personal secretary, had, among other duties, the privilege of decoding certain top-secret documents Madame Ngha would show to no one else. Though Van was in her complete confidence, her position was not exactly a relaxed one. Her boss was sometimes given to quick changes of temper that could make her harsh and even unjust. Yet Madame Ngha almost always regretted them, and when she realized her error immediately apologized with such charm that Van was unable to hold it against her.

The secretary was at this moment bent over her desk, flipping through a thick dictionary and checking various papers as she scribbled in a notebook. Thick glasses aged her and gave her the air of a schoolmistress correcting her pupils' homework.

'It's very long,' she said. 'I've finished, but the rough copy is illegible and I'm in the process of recopying it. Do you want to see these first pages?'

'No. You know perfectly well I prefer having the finished work.... But do you think it's interesting?'

Absorbed in the mechanical details of decoding, Van had not been able to appreciate the content of the message, though certain passages had struck her.

'Some of the information seems quite interesting. The rest less so, I think.'

'Finish it quickly.'

This conversation took place not far from Hanoi, in a secluded corner of the Vietnamese countryside fixed up to serve as the main quarters of the Democratic Republic's General Intelligence Service. The accommodation was not luxurious, but the underground bunkers were solidly built. All the same, the officials of the service found means to live there comfortably enough as well as a tranquillity that favoured subtle schemes and well-deliberated decisions; when, that is, enemy aircraft did not bomb too close by. Even if the offices were not equipped with the latest refinements of Western technology, the information converging there was no less abundant and valuable. The brains that analysed it, less rapidly, perhaps, but with more discrimination than computers, knew how to turn it to the best possible advantage. Madame Ngha was one of these—the most important of all.

She was for the moment unoccupied, which happened rarely, and with her chin in her hands tried not to show too much impatience as she waited for Van to finish deciphering the long message just received from one of her agents operating in enemy territory. Only once did she interrupt her meditations, opening her mouth as if to say something. Then she changed her mind, considering it useless to distract her secretary once again, and instead silently noted on a pad:

—Instructions to send to Thu: Henceforth, for long reports sent by messenger, no longer transcribe into code. Waste of time at point of transmission as well as reception, and completely unnecessary. If such a long text falls into enemy hands, they will always manage to decipher it.—

She knew the enemy's resources in this field and hated nothing more than a fruitless waste of time. Although occasionally delighting in intrigues of rare complexity, she appreciated simplicity in matters where no disadvantage would result.

Like her secretary she was dressed indistinctively in a loose-fitting jacket and trousers that could just as well have been civilian as military. Two identical caps hung on bamboo pegs at the entrance to the room. Also like Van, she wore no military stripes or insignia. But there the resemblance ended. Van was a young Vietnamese girl from Hanoi, indistinguishable from her sisters except for her glasses with their abnormally thick lenses, while Madame Ngha, despite her frequent efforts to pass unnoticed, never completely succeeded in hiding beneath an apparent nonchalance the radiance of her gaze and the extraordinary intelligence emanating from her face. Her stature also made her conspicuous—taller than most Vietnamese women, she was slimmer than Van, though certainly much older. She undoubtedly owed some of these characteristics to her parents' intermarriage: her mother was Chinese, from Shanghai. No one would risk a guess at her age. She carried herself like a young girl; her face, though paler and more elongated that Van's, was as smooth, and her hair, cut short like the Chinese, contributed to her air of youthfulness. Her expression, however, was one of maturity, and the position she occupied had been entrusted to her only after she had given proof of her wisdom and experience over the course of many years.

Madame Ngha held one of the highest positions in the Democratic Republic. A privileged few, in the complete confidence of Uncle Ho, knew she was the supreme head of the intelligence services. Others—especially the soldiers with whom she frequently mingled while intent on making her own inquiries at every level—even if unaware of her exact functions and rank in the hierarchy, were still able to divine in her a figure of considerable distinction, laden with heavy responsibilities and sufficiently enigmatic, despite her good-natured manner and familiarity, to satisfy their innate love of mystery and intrigue. They also knew she was very close to the President and enjoyed his absolute confidence. Along the pathways and trails of the jungle where the convoys moved at night, certain words attributed to Uncle Ho were quoted on occasion. It was said he had declared one day that he would rather see the city of Hanoi reduced to ashes by B-52's than be deprived of Madame Ngha.

Thus, in speaking of her, the soldiers gave her a now-outmoded title; she was never called *Comrade* Ngha. Occasionally, of course, she would be referred to by a sobriquet, like 'Shimmering Light' or 'More Subtle than the Musk Deer', earned by the radiance of her eyes and the resourcefulness of her mind. For some people, depending on their age, their position in the hierarchy, or their degree of intimacy, she might also be 'Aunt Ngha' or 'Big Sister Ngha'. But most often, for the people, and especially the soldiers, she was Ba Ngha, Madame Ngha, and this is the name that had finally stuck. Even in the highest circles and the very bosom of the Party, she was referred to in this way, half in jest, half seriously, but always with a tinge of respect—Madame Ngha.

'At last!'

She seized the report held out by her secretary. It began:

—'Thu to her dear Aunt Ngha ...'

She had begun to read under her breath, then stopped and lifting her eyes caught a glimmer of amusement on Van's face. A tender smile hovered on her own and more as a matter of form she asked: 'What is it, Van?'

'I'm wondering if the enemy intelligence service receives reports from its secret agents beginning like that.'

'I doubt it. But that's Thu—she needs to create a family atmosphere around her.' She continued to read:

—'Am assigned new service directed by General Bishop.

Reasons to think service very important. First here precise details.

—'Geographical position: East Thailand. Longitude 104° 17'. Latitude 16° 33'. Right beside existing B-52 base. Large airfield. Fuel and munitions depot. Sending details soonest possible. Been here only eight days.

—'Our service: Shrouded in mystery not yet completely penetrated. Believe however beginning to discover objective. (See last part present report.) Official name: Service S. Know now S initial for Sensors.* Not found word in dictionary but think know meaning (see last part).

—'Buildings: One very large room (at a glance about 100 × 30, but unable to measure. Sorry. Have as yet only been inside once) called monitoring room, with adjoining offices for officers in charge, in particular General Bishop's office, which will also be mine. General Bishop wants me near him. Has complete confidence in me.

—'Quarters: Pleasant and comfortable for all personnel, including myself. Bungalow type.... Dear Aunt Ngha, I have a bathroom, a refrigerator, air conditioning, a large living room just for me, and a garden, small, but where I have had the pleasure of discovering three hibiscus almost as beautiful as those in Hue....'

'Thu will always be the same,' Madame Ngha commented with another fond smile. 'Has she really taken the time and trouble to translate "Dear Aunt Ngha" into code?'

'She has. I've also noticed she frequently abandons the telegraphic style,' Van remarked.

'When she thinks that what she has to say is better expressed otherwise.'

—'... As I was able to wander about during this first week, when I've been on a sort of vacation, I've also had the immense joy of discovering a river, smaller than the Perfumed River but a bit reminiscent of it. However, what follows will no doubt interest you more, my dear Aunt Ngha.

* The *sensors* are described in detail in the *Armed Forces Journal* of February 15, 1971. They are artificial sensing devices.

—'Personnel: First, General Bishop. He is a well-bred American....'

3

Van interpreted the fact that Madame Ngha had again paused and heaved a sigh as a token of disapproval, and thought she might take the opportunity to add a few remarks.

'At first Thu really tries to be methodical. She begins by expressing herself in a precise and condensed style. But then she strays into descriptions and digressions that have almost nothing to do with the facts, so that before reaching the main point, since she gives the most important information at the end, she gets carried away—by her temperament, no doubt....'

'That *is* her temperament, Van, but I don't regard it as a fault. I feel that each agent must be allowed to express himself according to his own individual nature, and all these digressions, as you call them, might one day be valuable. In any case, I'm delighted to know Thu is in pleasant surroundings. She will be more at ease there and I'm sure her work will benefit. Do you know her background?'

'Only from her dossier. I've never met her. Wasn't she a war orphan?'

'Her entire family was massacred in an American bombardment near Hue. She wasn't even fifteen. Afterwards she fought with the Vietcong commandos for a while, where she gave ample proof of her resolution and courage. But it went against her nature—brutality revolted her sensibilities. She simply wasn't made for witnessing atrocities, much less for participating in them. I understood that immediately when I met her one day by accident in the course of one of my first tours of the trail; her eyes were wide with horror: she had just been on a punitive commando operation. Even after her sufferings, and with hatred for the enemy in her heart, she still couldn't stand the sight of just executions. I gained her confidence. It was easy; a few friendly words were enough. She told me her life story and all her misfortunes, which made me think she could be much more useful in my intelligence service.... She possesses that quality most precious in a secret agent: she inspires confidence. With the appealing face of a slightly melancholy child, refined and delicate like the girls of Hue.... But Van, what's the matter?'

Madame Ngha, sensitive to every nuance, had noticed a slight flutter of the eyelashes behind the thick lenses, perhaps the expression of a certain agitation provoked by Madame Ngha's moving description of Thu and the obvious conclusion that this gentle creature was to become a top-rate agent, exposed to the most awful brutalities and even violent death if things should turn out badly.

'Nothing, Madame, nothing,' she replied hastily.

Madame Ngha shook her head and went on: 'So I asked the Vietcong to transfer her to us and by intrigue managed to have her enlisted by the Americans. She spoke English fairly fluently and her charm and simplicity made things easier. She has already performed services for us as secretary and translator in an enemy command post. She will perform others. But I repeat: for her equanimity it is essential that she does not live in a grim atmosphere.'

'It seemed to me that her reflections on the character of this General Bishop ...'

'They could prove to be important. Personally, I'm glad to know this general is a well-bred American. I'm pleased first of all for Thu, who will be decently treated if she can escape the dangers constantly threatening her, and secondly for us, since you can never know the enemy too well.... "Know the enemy, know yourself"* must be our rule at all times. Have you forgotten that? Thu knows it instinctively, and

* Giap, *People's Army, People's War*.

14

for what you call her digressions I consider her a remarkable agent. Wouldn't you agree with me?'

Her attitude had changed imperceptibly and her tone hardened almost to the point of severity. Although, to be sure, she tolerated discussion and even contradiction, once she had provided her secretary with, to her mind, irrefutable reasons for her judgment, she considered continuing the conversation a waste of time.

'I never claimed otherwise,' declared Van in a contrite tone. 'I simply wanted to say that the essential information was at the end.'

'Really?'

Madame Ngha calmly resumed her reading:

—'PERSONNEL: First, General Bishop. He is a well-bred American. He does not drink much and rarely smokes, and then only a pipe. He is correct and even deferential towards me, the only girl in the department. If he has vices, they are well hidden, but I will do my best to discover them and send details. He seems highly honoured to have been placed at the head of Service S. I have not yet been able to find out his exact age, but he is no longer particularly young, though well preserved, and I have heard rumours that this will probably be his last assignment before retirement.

—'In this connection I must report here some information gathered while listening to odd conversations among the staff, who speak quite freely in front of me. I cannot guarantee this information since it has not been double-checked. According to some, General Bishop's appointment to this post was due to his professional conscience and industry. Others add: to his total ignorance of the workings of the department he has to direct. As the department is composed of engineers and technicians, the military high command deemed it necessary to have an officer superior to functional matters to take over-all responsibility. One of these engineers, who is very young, mentioned with an apparently ironic smile the "Peter Principle". I am sorry I don't understand, and will try to find out....'

'Do you know, Van, what is meant by the Peter Principle?'

Van humbly admitted she did not.

'Well, it would be wise to keep yourself better informed in the future. Remind me to give you the book by Peter and Hull this evening and read it, as I have, carefully.'

Van leaned over and jotted it down in her notebook. Madame Ngha continued:

—'... In the opinion of still others (excuse the length of this paragraph, but I think these matters might be important) in the opinion of others, Bishop was appointed to this coveted post (Thailand is sought after by all the American officers) because, although capable of taking initiative, he would never interfere with the operation of the computers, which are essential to the functioning of Service S (see last part). The entire staff is proud to have an IBM S 360/65 here, which is apparently a wonder and unbelievably expensive.

—'I think in concluding this paragraph that my dear Aunt Ngha would like to know my personal opinion of General Bishop. I am sorry that it is still very vague. At this moment, I can only say he is old enough to be my father ...'

'She's in just the right place beside this old general,' murmured Madame Ngha.

—'... old enough to be my father, and less unsympathetic than many of the young officers; not exactly naïve, but appears to have a great admiration for things he doesn't understand properly, such as science and technology. (Thu is very sorry for the imprecision of this judgment. She will try to be better informed in the next report.)

—'Colonel Shaw, number two, adjutant to the general ...'

'There, despite the vagueness, is at least a character sketch,' commented Madame Ngha, apparently delighted with these lines. 'And you maintained that these details were unimportant! Believe me—they're neither a waste of time nor paper.'

—'... is easier to define. Physicist. Electronics expert, with officer's stripes pinned on him. Mocks them and uninterested in the war....'

'There, she's back to a telegraphic style.'

'Not for long.'

—'... Has passion only for his speciality and proper functioning of GADGETS (word he uses) invented and perfected by him, basis of Service S (see last part). Does not seem concerned about military consequences gadgets might entail. Thu sometimes imagines state of mind resembling that of atomic physicists Los Alamos.

—'OTHER MEMBERS OF STAFF: All engineers and technicians often as not speaking incomprehensible language. Thu apologizes again. I might, however, have got a faint idea of the nature of Service S, due to begin operation next week, from a conversation between Colonel Shaw and the general (who doesn't understand technical language either, so the colonel had to explain things to him in plain English) and from some details the general gave me on his own. (I have already mentioned he has complete confidence in me. He wants to make me his personal secretary, which could be very useful for my work.)

—'PART TWO: BASIC OBJECTIVE OF SERVICE S AND NATURE OF SENSORS: These SENSORS are instruments that pick up sound. Failing to find a translation in Vietnamese, I have called them *ears of the jungle*. You will see why....'

' "Ears of the jungle," ' Madame Ngha murmured thoughtfully. 'I suppose this is the second part containing the main point you referred to.'

'Exactly. Very interesting, but at the same time very disturbing.'

Madame Ngha read the last part of the report without a break, then went back to the beginning and reread it more slowly, pausing to frown at certain passages. When she had finished she looked at her secretary with appreciation.

'You were right, Van,' she said. 'Here's the main point, at least for the moment. Interesting, but very disturbing. However, thanks to Thu we've been forewarned. We'll have to put our own brains to work to find a response to this....

In the meantime, we must reply today and thank her properly. All right. . . .'

While Van prepared to obey, Madame Ngha got up and started to pace the office, hands behind her back. She now looked like a businessman pondering the various aspects of a problem before dictating an important letter, hesitating between several possible formulations. After a few moments of deep thought, this supreme and often awesome head of the intelligence service suddenly made up her mind, and began: 'Ready, Van :—Ngha to her very dear young sister, Thu—'

4

Nam was relaxed at the wheel of his three-ton truck that, though patched up several times, was still solid. He felt at ease despite the treacherousness of this part of the trail where for some months now he had practised his skill at driving. This section, about eighteen miles long, was not one of the most dangerous; the enemy did not appear to have located it yet. Nam had been bombed only twice, and the explosives, dropped rather haphazardly, it seemed, had not hit his convoy. The real difficulty lay in driving the vehicles.

No one in his right mind would have dreamed these mountains covered in dense forest could be crossed by columns of trucks like Nam's. Yet almost every night they managed to thread their way along the narrow trails so crudely hacked through the dense growth of trees and creepers, invisible from the sky. Indeed, trucks of three tons were the limit. Heavier ones had certainly been tried—in fact, every conceivable means of transport had been experimented with—but they had all had to be given up. Twisted frames at the bottoms of the ravines recalled the presumptuousness of such attempts.

But the three-tonners made it, driven by virtual acrobats at the wheel who had had to undergo incredibly gruelling tests before being entrusted with supply-laden trucks bound for the troops operating in the south. These vehicles and supplies were more precious than gold. Once approved, each of these élite drivers was assigned a fifteen- to twenty-mile stretch of the trail from which he was never moved, so that as he became familiar with every hazard—the sharp tyre-slashing rocks, the ruts, the tiniest roots—he could almost have driven it blindfold.

It mattered little that the drivers were not blind, for transport was always carried out at night and without a single light that could attract pilots. Their reactions were triggered solely by a close contact with the rugged ground maintained through the wheels and transmission, forming a circuit that was by now almost an integral part of Nam's nervous system. He was satisfied with his lot: his assignment, though difficult, was less perilous here than on many of the other wider and better-laid trails, where the bombings were more frequent and effective.

On this particular night Nam had further reason to rejoice: he had a promotion to be proud of. For the first time he had been chosen to drive the truck at the head of the convoy, a tribute to his proficiency, for it was by far the most delicate task. Even on the darkest night, in passages over which the giant trees knitted their branches to form an opaque curtain between the earth and the faint glow of the tropical sky, the ordinary truck driver could always make out some faint indication of the vehicle in front, provided he followed closely enough. For the drivers it had become a game of reflexes. Two trucks, one following the other, seemed bound by intangible, tenuous nerves like elastic threads hardly more than a yard long. Whenever the elastic tended to stretch farther, the driver of the second truck, just at the moment when the vague signs of the vehicle ahead were about to disappear, would press imperceptibly on the accelerator, then abruptly but equally unconsciously, though always with the same precise judgment, on the brake as the dark mass suddenly loomed, warning him the thread was lax and a crash imminent. The drivers' dexterity was such that collisions almost never occurred

But tonight Nam, at the head of the column, could not rely on these signals. He was so familiar with the trail, however, that he managed to follow it at a fairly even speed without losing his way and still avoid most of the hazards. He rarely needed the help of the co-driver seated to his right, who leaned his head out of the window to warn him of unforeseen obstacles. Behind, the convoy progressed at a moderate but sustained pace, five or six miles an hour, furtively winding its way like a python beneath the foliage of the trees.

It was an important convoy, which added to Nam's pride. The departure had been shrouded in mystery and the final orders issued only at the last minute. The authorities were apprehensive and Nam had known it. Although he concentrated on the trail and its hazards, he could not prevent himself from occasionally mulling over the many changes in the plans for their departure. The itinerary had been decided on two days before, and he and his companions had been ready and waiting. The day after, the order had been cancelled and another route designated; then finally, at the last moment, he had been requested to start out. It was clear to him the authorities feared trouble. Recollecting an incident from previous days, he thought he could guess at least part of the reason for this uneasiness.

The week before, on moonless nights, a large number of enemy aircraft had flown over the region. By the mysterious telegraph that crossed Vietnam from north to south, Nam knew the same thing had happened the whole length of the Annamite chain, from the through passes up to Dalat, from the edge of the sea across to Laos and Cambodia. It was certainly not the first time, but several anomalies made these flights incomprehensible. The aircraft were not bombers: they had released no explosives. They seemed to fly in perfect formation, passing regularly back and forth as if wishing to rake each acre of the high country from above. Spotters? The nights were dark, and even with the enemy's fiendish methods observation was difficult. Besides, not a single flare had been dropped. Paratroops? Impossible over the jungle at night. Delayed-action bombs? To Nam this was still the least absurd possibility. Yet on reflection it too appeared preposterous. If that's what it was, the Americans were even more insane than he had thought until then. The jungle was huge, and they could never cover its surface with enough devices to be disturbing, despite the superabundance of their matériel. Dropped at night from a high altitude, there was a good chance that none had fallen on a trail used by the convoys.

All the same, the authorities must have envisaged this possibility, since patrols had been sent out into the jungle in practically every direction. Patrols of experts. Nam had seen one of them coming back from its investigations and could have sworn the soldiers who composed it were not real soldiers. In any case, judging from their expressions, he was sure they had returned empty-handed. The whole thing seemed rather mysterious, and he experienced a slight, not unpleasant thrill.

Still musing to himself, he thought: If bad luck puts one of these damned contraptions in our path, mine will certainly be the first to get it. Shrugging his shoulders, he brushed these thoughts aside and, without diverting his attention from the driving, began to dream of the break he was due at the next stopover, where the convoy would be taken over by other drivers for the next stage of its nocturnal journey. The stopover was a fortified position with secure shelters that the authorities had taken equal care to make a place of rest and relaxation for the hard-working drivers and passing troops. There were fairly well-stocked shops and recreation rooms.

Nam smiled with pleasure at the recollection of some of the amusements they offered.

The smile spread and a gleam shone in his eye as his dreams took another direction. He now imagined himself one day telling his grandchildren how he had been appointed head of a convoy on the Ho Chi Minh Trail. He would be respected by everyone then.

The co-driver tensed slightly and craned his neck out of the window.

'*Mai bai!*'*

He blew a succession of strident blasts on his whistle, which immediately reverberated the length of the convoy. Nam braked savagely and switched off the engine. He was promptly imitated by all the drivers in the column stretched out over several hundred yards. He now distinctly heard the sound of aircraft but wasn't terribly worried, since flights overhead were a common enough occurrence. Silent and immobile under cover of the jungle, especially dense at this point, the convoy could not be spotted from the sky even if the enemy dropped flares. Usually, after a similar alarm, the roar of airplane engines receded and the convoy continued its tortuous, serpentine progress.

This time, however, the airplanes were not far away and coming closer. The roar increased each second, as if ... as if, Nam thought suddenly, seeking the gaze of his co-driver in the darkness ... as if the aircraft were headed straight for them, unerringly and without the least hesitation. He glimpsed the same fear in his companion: the anguish of being a target.

'They're aiming straight for us,' said the co-driver.

He had to shout to make himself heard above the deafening roar. The planes must have been almost directly overhead, and the men's experience of air raids in the north enabled them to recognize the characteristic sound of dive bombers.

* 'Airplanes!'

'I tell you, they've spotted us!'

'Impossible,' replied Nam, now leaning his head out of the window. 'The night's pitch black. There's not a single light on us. They ...'

The blast of the first bombs cut him short. At the same instant he saw behind him the invisible serpent metamorphose into a dragon of fire.

5

'Regulations were followed,' Nam confirmed. 'I know because I looked back just before the first bombs hit. There wasn't a single light, not even the glow of a cigarette.'

Daybreak revealed the smoking debris of the convoy lying in the midst of disfigured jungle: mangled trucks, protruding pieces of jagged metal, gutted sacks of rice, and a few odd vehicles still on their wheels were about all that remained. Only Nam and a few of his comrades had come through unscathed. Medical orderlies were giving first aid to the wounded stretched out on the ground. Mutilated corpses, some of them charred, were scattered here and there along the trail, now scarred by craters of varying sizes. All the munitions bound for troops in the south had exploded.

Two Vietnamese, a man and a woman, explored the disaster, commenting on its extent and expressing their rage only in an occasional curl of the lip. An escort of soldiers armed with submachine guns and carrying grenades on their belts stood guard, not letting the couple out of their sight for an instant. They were both high-ranking officials.

One was General Hoan, in charge of transport for this sector of the Ho Chi Minh Trail. His command post was only about forty miles away, and he had considered the incident serious enough, as much for the incomprehensible circumstances of the raid as the extent of the damage, to come and inspect for himself. The woman was even more important than Hoan. It was Madame Ngha. She had been making a tour a little to the north of the seventeenth parallel when she had been informed of this unusual attack. She too had instantly modified her itinerary and, in order to see for herself, crossed the frontier and penetrated deep into the southern zone.

Dressed in her usual sober manner and wearing the ubiquitous cap, from which not a single strand of hair escaped, her rank in the hierarchy was only apparent in General Hoan's deference and the size of the escort he had mobilized specifically for her protection the moment she had informed him of her arrival. This was not common practice. Generals, and even more important people, often moved about with an ordinary guard of a few men. Madame Ngha herself required only the attendance of her faithful Van, who followed her like a shadow, laden with a briefcase stuffed with documents and a miniature communicator that operated on a secret wavelength. She and three or four soldiers, one of whom carried the bedding, made up her usual entourage. But Hoan, by nature anxious and already unreasonably fearful he would be allotted some responsibility for the loss of the convoy, was taking no chances. He would find it uncomfortable in high places if Madame Ngha met with an accident on the trail. Hence he had given orders of such severity that none of the soldiers in the escort dared take his eyes off her.

'Not a single light,' repeated the driver Nam. 'I know because I deliberately checked when I realized we were the target.'

'It's all right,' Madame Ngha said to him, 'you have given proof of your cool-headedness and intelligence. I congratulate you on saving your truck as well.'

She offered him a cigarette, which Nam lit with a swagger. It was true. He had shown great presence of mind and saved his truck. Seeing the convoy in flames, he had remained

tupefied for only a second. Then, to escape the blaze spread-
ng rapidly from vehicle to vehicle as well as the continuous
ain of bombs, he had restarted the engine and, jamming down
he accelerator, bounded desperately forward into the now
rightly lit jungle. He had succeeded in covering several hun-
lred yards this way and finally hurled his truck off the trail
etween two trees, protecting it from the blasts.

After interrogating a few other survivors and being convinced that the security regulations had been obeyed, General
Hoan summed up the situation as he saw it.

'At night, in this jungle, such precision is incomprehensible.'

Madame Ngha, who detested the word incomprehensible,
grimaced slightly.

'Look,' he insisted, 'all the bombs fell in alignment with our
invisible trail. I sent patrols all around and the number of
craters quickly diminishes as you get farther away. Hardly a
single bomb wasted. It's the same in front and behind the convoy—almost nothing. They aimed at it as if through sights.'

'I see,' she said in a rather cool tone.

'They must have been informed precisely, almost to the
second, of the convoy's departure, its exact route. We've been
betrayed—there's hardly any doubt of that.'

There was a respectful hint of reproach in his words, as if
he chief of intelligence, of espionage and counterespionage
ought to have some share in the responsibility for this affair.

'I assume,' she remarked in an even cooler tone, 'that you
didn't proclaim in advance the time of departure and route
chosen. I assume the indispensable security regulations for a
convoy of this importance were also applied by you and your
colleagues.'

'Without a doubt,' the general replied hastily. 'I spoke fool-
ishly. Of course a betrayal by someone on our side is impossible. The actual route remained confidential until the last
minute and the drivers were informed only at the exact
moment of departure. The secret was known only to me and
my chief of staff.'

'And I again assume that he is as much above suspicion a
yourself.'

The general blushed, stammered, and looked almost guilty
However, his innocence was not in question and she wa
well aware of that. Assigned to the important post he occupie
because of his very real organizational abilities, he carried ou
his duties competently and with zeal. But his reflection
irritated her. She reproached him with a lack of assurance—
and the onset of a certain obesity; quite unfairly, howevei
since this was due to deficient health and not high living,
fact not unknown to her. She was in a difficult mood, though
and when that was the case, the most innocent and self
possessed man in the world might have been disconcerted.

But she did not abuse her victory, simply continuing: 'A
you see ... a betrayal by one of us wouldn't explain the almos
miraculous precision of the raid, which you have just analyse
so perceptively.'

They took a few more steps along the trail, moving from
the wreckage of one truck to another, closely followed by the
guard. The damage was terrible; three-quarters of the convo
annihilated. The wreckage now lay in broad daylight as th
sun's rays unnaturally pierced the jungle through gaps tor
in the foliage by the explosions. All the smaller trees wer
slashed to pieces and the large ones riddled with wounds an
stained with variegated sap.

'The rice that can still be used must be collected,' she said
pointing to some half-disembowelled sacks, 'and the fev
trucks worth repairing should be salvaged. We are short o
vehicles.'

She had sufficient authority to interfere at times in matter
that bore little relation to her own department. The genera
showed no inclination to object.

'I have already given orders. A team will arrive tonight.'

They had just completed their dismal tour when the jungl
suddenly resounded with guttural cries. The soldiers immedi

ately raised their weapons and formed a circle around them. The uproar continued: shouts, a furious chase—it sounded like a manhunt.

And so it was, a manhunt led by soldiers of a patrol sent out on reconnaissance by Hoan. They soon came into view, pushing before them a prisoner. It was Mok, the Jarai chief. They had deprived him of his gun, his machete, and even his flashlight. The noncommissioned officer in command of the patrol reported to the general.

'There are others, but they escaped us. They slither through the creepers like eels.'

Mok's advanced age had prevented him from making good his escape like the other tribesmen, who were much swifter in the forest than the most agile of the soldiers.

'Shall I have them pursued?' asked the officer.

He was about to give the order at a sign from Hoan when Madame Ngha cut in impatiently: 'Stop, and recall all your men.'

An order from her was not open to discussion. Simply as a matter of form the NCO's eyes sought his chief's confirmation, which was not long in coming. Meanwhile Madame Ngha tried to help him save face.

'With your permission, General, I suggest these men be left alone. They are harmless and could be very useful to us if we treat them properly.'

'I'll do as you say. But—harmless? I myself believe they were here spying on us, just waiting for our departure to loot what's left of the convoy. At least we've captured one of them.'

'I don't think they are looters. I also suggest your men free this old man and give him back his gun. I know him.'

'You know him?'

'Yes, I know him. Again, with your permission, I shall offer him your apologies.'

The general grudgingly gave his soldiers the order. Mok was freed. He had remained motionless and rather aloof during this conversation in Vietnamese, of which he did not

27

understand a word, guessing only that it concerned him.

Madame Ngha smiled and looked him straight in the eyes, then began: *'Tam cho oi ...'**

General Hoan was so stupefied he could not even utter an exclamation. The soldiers all stared in amazement. Madame Ngha had spoken in a strange language that was obviously Jarai, since the old chief's face, at first as surprised as the rest, gradually cleared. She paused briefly, as if to enjoy the sensation produced on her retinue, and then continued with apparent ease, though her lilting intonation occasionally drew a smile from the tribesman.

'Don't you recognize me? I visited you several moons ago in your new village. You had just set up your houses. You received me well then. I brought you the greetings of our great chief and assurances on his behalf that you had nothing to fear from us. We have kept our word, and we will always keep it. I even remember your name. Mok and his brothers have nothing to fear.'

The old man bowed several times before her.

'I recognize you,' he said. 'It really was you who came. But we needed an interpreter to understand each other then.'

'You see I can now do without an interpreter.'

For the past few years the leaders of the Democratic Republic had felt that the tribes of hill people haunting the Annamite chain—the Jarai, Rhade, Sedang, Maa, and several others, till then regarded as *moïs*—savages—deserved to be taken into consideration. They could play a useful role in the war, and their good will was to be sought.

It had not always been that way. In the past, not long after the Geneva accords, the North Vietnamese leaders had treated the unfortunate *moïs* in almost as scornful, if not as cruel, a manner as had the Diem clique in the south. There, too, whole families had been uprooted from their homes and deported. But times had changed. Madame Ngha especially, as soon as she had been given an important post, struggled against these policies, judging them clumsy and ineffective as

* 'Oh Grandfather ...' (very respectful form of address).

28

well as barbarous. It was partly thanks to her influence that Uncle Ho's policies regarding the hill tribesmen had been modified.

A few months previously, considering the problem important enough to justify personal contact, she had in fact secretly visited several villages in the high country, and Mok's in particular, accompanied by her secretary, an interpreter, and a few bodyguards.

Their meeting had been courteous. She had drunk rice wine with them and conferred with Mok and certain of the notables, making an effort to put them at their ease and create a bond of friendship. Ami had not put in an appearance that day, remaining shuttered in her hut throughout the visit, listening carefully and watching the eyes of the Vietnamese woman through the bamboo. Her impression was favourable, but she preferred to await future events before forming a definite opinion.

It was after this trip that Madame Ngha had decided to learn the language of these people, convinced it would one day be useful to her. Within a few months, at a speed that said a great deal for her powers of assimilation, she had acquired a decent knowledge of Jarai to add to her perfect command of Chinese, Russian, French and English, as well as a smattering of each of the dialects spoken in the Indochinese peninsula.

'Mok and his brothers have nothing to fear,' she insisted. 'You must excuse these soldiers. They are only performing their duty, for, as you know, we are at war and always have to be on our guard. They took you and your companions for thieves come to pillage the little that remains of our convoy.'

'We are not thieves,' said Mok, raising his head proudly.

'I know, and I have explained that.'

Once again Mok bowed before her, happy to have been understood.

'I knew perfectly well they had not come to plunder,' she said to General Hoan.

'What are they doing here then?'

'He is just about to tell me.'

Anxious to justify the trust shown in him, the tribal chief resumed of his own accord: 'We are not thieves. We are farmers and sometimes hunters.'

'Yes, I know.'

'And it is the hunters who are here this morning, myself and the men from the village. But then, it's a long story....'

'Tell me, if you would,' she said, squatting on her heels in peasant fashion and motioning him to do likewise. 'But first, if you trust me, call your companions back. I would like them to fraternize with the Vietnamese soldiers so they can see that we're all friends.'

The old man did not hesitate for a moment. He turned towards the forest and, cupping his hands to his mouth, let out several guttural cries, interspersing them with a stream of words. These she followed without too much difficulty and translated for the general. The chief ordered all of his men to return and bring with them what it was they had come in search of, in order to prove conclusively that they were not in any way convoy thieves.

6

Not the least rustle betrayed their approach as the Jarai appeared one by one in response to Mok's summons. He addressed a few more words to them and they all bowed down before Madame Ngha, laying at her feet the bloodstained bodies of an enormous boar, its feet attached to a pole, and two wild pigs.

'Is that all?' demanded Mok.

'That's all. We've scoured the jungle around the craters. There's nothing else.'

'This is what we came here to look for,' declared the old man. 'The animals belong to the jungle and those who capture them. It is not proper hunting, but it is not theft.'

'I understand,' said Madame Ngha.

'It is not our normal way of hunting,' insisted the chief, 'but ...'

He was determined to give a full explanation in order to clear his people of any suspicions that might still hover over the object of their expedition. It was clear, too, that he sought to excuse himself and his companions for this rather humiliating way of capturing game. He spoke at great length and somewhat slowly, to be better understood by the Vietnamese woman, who listened with visible interest, occasionally interrupting to have him repeat a word she did not quite grasp and even comment on its meaning, if necessary.

Several times during his account she nodded her head approvingly and at times gave way to a smile. Whenever Mok paused to catch his breath she would summarize his confidences in a few well-chosen words. Though this translation was meant to enlighten Hoan, it was obvious it was principally for the soldiers' benefit, and provoked among them a mute enthusiasm. Her account so excited and intrigued them that they completely forgot their orders and, in their desire to hear better, drew gradually closer until at last they too were squatting, in a wholly democratic manner, around the group. Now and then shouts of glee escaped them, despite the reproving eye of the general, who, however, dared not intervene, so readily did Madame Ngha appear to accept and even encourage this familiarity.

Mok's speech, though long and studded with digressions on the present difficulties of the hill people, was essentially the statement of a quite simple system, worked out by primitive minds on the basis of the obvious.

For a long time the inhabitants of the high region had noticed, sometimes to their cost, that the stones dropped from the sky by the flying men were lethal. The fact that they were also fatal to the North Vietnamese and their convoys left them basically rather indifferent. This was not their war and besides, their native land was the jungle. They could hardly be expected to wax enthusiastic about ideologies they found incomprehensible. Far more important to them was the remark made by Ami as early as the first raid: If fire stones kill men, they will also slaughter wild beasts.

At first, though, they had been assailed by an unspoken anxiety, the fear of seeing their precious game, the essential nourishment on whose reproduction the future of their children depended, annihilated. But the jungle was vast, as Ami often repeated, and despite the hail of stones pounding it each night, a great many more would be necessary to cause the disappearance of its animal life. The game, which was what interested the hunters, certainly had far more room than the inhabitants of a city (the Jarai, who sometimes manoeuvred for weeks to approach a herd of buffalo, knew that all too well), and if the bombings had never succeeded in destroying the entire population of a city, there was all the more reason to suppose that most of the animals would survive.

Just the same, the explosives frequently took a few isolated victims, and if by any chance a spirit directed them into the vicinity of a herd, the haul might be considerable. It would be a shame to let it go to waste.

'It is not really hunting,' the old chief insisted, 'but it is better this meat should nourish our women and children than lie there and rot, or feed tigers, or wild dogs and scavengers.'

'That's very wise,' approved Madame Ngha.

'And there is also the excuse that game is scarce in these mountains where we've been forced to take refuge by the war. Our women and children very often go hungry.'

So it was that the Jarai hunters had begun to follow the flights of American bombers over the Annamite chain with increasing interest: a specific interest, very different from that of combatants. On the nights when a distant drone announced

32

a raid by the flying men, it was accompanied by the fervent hopes of the hill tribesmen, longing from the depths of their naïve souls for the deadly stones to fall not too far from their village and in a region rich with game.

'When that happens,' said the old man, reassured by the kindly attitude of his listeners, 'despite these hard times we often sacrifice a chicken and a jar of rice wine to the *yangs*, and say the hunter's prayer, the one that goes:

'O spirits of the village, of the fields, of the lakes, we depart for the hunt and want to share game among us. O mountain spirits, spirits of the rocks, let us capture the wild animals without difficulty.'*

When their hopes, their sacrifices, or their prayers had been answered, or at least when they figured there was a good chance they might have been, an expedition was mounted to the scene of the slaughter, made up of a larger or smaller number of men, depending on the quantity of spoils they hoped to bring back.

Today the bag had not been large: a boar and two wild pigs. Nevertheless, it had not been a complete failure, as had sometimes happened before, since this type of hunt was risky and the men had often known the humiliation of returning to the village with a mutilated giant lizard the only spoil.

'Have you sometimes had good catches?'

With an exclamation the chief related how one night, after a prayer more fervent than usual, the firestones had fallen right in the middle of a herd of deer. At dawn eight good-sized animals had been found, and they had had to send to the village for reinforcements to carry them all back.

'We filled several large earthenware jars with their meat, and the village feasted for weeks.'

Another time—now there was no hint of weariness as Mok recounted their exploits—another time some stones had

* *Jarai Prayers.*

fallen in a river teeming with fish, fortunately not very far from their village.

'It was I who understood they had struck the water, for the night before I had dreamed I was catching chickens.'

'Chickens?'

'To us that means you are going to catch many fish. So I recited the fisherman's prayer myself, the one that begins:

'O Spirits—I set upon the water the canoe, the raft. Cause the fish to come to me, that I may easily catch a great number, and let me do so without fatigue, without hardship.'*

Van regarded her chief with astonishment, knowing how much she loathed wasting her time. Madame Ngha was listening to the old man recite these invocations in a harsh tongue without showing the slightest sign of impatience. On the contrary, she seemed to derive great pleasure from this and refrained from interrupting to translate the main points of his narrative.

'... then again I had the happy idea of directing the men, not towards the spot where the stones had dropped, but farther downstream, to a place where the river broadens out to form a peaceful lake. That's where we put our rafts in the water.'

His prediction was right. They had collected pounds and pounds of large fish, enough to fill ten huge baskets and give their menu some variety.

'But a windfall like that is rare,' he concluded modestly. 'What a shame,' he added, pointing towards the west, 'what a shame the stones didn't fall a little farther away last night, over there, on the Plain of a Hundred Thousand Buffalo. With a little luck more game would have been slaughtered than we could have carried away.'

'Really?' asked Madame Ngha, who seemed to become more and more aroused by these revelations. 'Really, the plain is that well stocked with game?'

* *Jarai Prayers.*

34

'That it is. The finest herds in the mountains are to be found there. If only the *yangs* had been favourable, there would have been enough for us and all your soldiers as well.'

At these words Madame Ngha became thoughtful for a while. She was only brought out of her reverie by a gesture from Mok, who pointed to the three beasts lying side by side on the ground.

'Today your soldiers must content themselves with this meagre offering, for though unworthy, it is yours. Accept it on behalf of the Jarai, with whom you know how to speak.'

'I cannot,' she protested. 'You told me the children of your village often go hungry. These animals are yours. Take them and give the children something to eat.'

There ensued a prolonged exchange of courtesies as the old man insisted and she refused this gift, while the hill tribesmen on one side and the soldiers on the other, their eyes shining with greed, awaited the outcome of the discussion not daring to intervene.

'The beasts of the jungle belong to him who finds them.'

'You speak the truth, but the one to whom they belong can make a present of them to anyone he pleases. And it was Dju, our best hunter, who found all three. I am sure he will agree with me and insist that you keep them too. ... Dju!'

Certain of the hunter's approval, he turned back towards his men and then frowned. Dju was not in the group.

'Where is Dju?'

The Jarai, quickly consulting among themselves in whispers, suddenly realized that no one had seen Dju for some time. He had stayed in the jungle and not responded to Mok's call. This was indeed unusual. The chief got up and shouted again and again at the top of his voice. After the third call, Dju's reply came from far away. He went on for quite a long time, while Mok listened carefully. Madame Ngha was unable to understand his explanations, since the sound was muffled by the distance and the brush; she had to ask Mok to repeat them.

'He says he has discovered an utterly foreign object, and does not want to take his eyes off it. He would like us to join him.'

7

The Jarai word Madame Ngha had translated roughly as 'foreign' seemed to her in need of some clarification.

'What is foreign to us,' Mok explained, 'is anything not belonging to the jungle.'

'Not belonging to the jungle?'

'That's what Dju meant. Maybe something has fallen from the sky. He dares not touch it.'

With a sudden frown and furtive glance at her secretary, Madame Ngha fully conveyed her interest in this discovery.

Disregarding his objections, she insisted that General Hoan alone accompany her; the soldiers were left behind surrounding the other hunters, still staring at them as if at some kind of natural wonder.

From time to time the old chief called out to Dju so that they could guide themselves by his response. The first steps were easy, as the undergrowth had been mangled and pulverized by the explosions. But gradually the network of plants and creepers reappeared. To facilitate the progress of the two Vietnamese, the hill tribesman had to resort to his machete. Madame Ngha seemed delighted with this excursion, but the general dripped with perspiration; he was panting by the time they finally reached Dju, who, crouched on his heels, was staring fixedly at a dense bush.

Not lifting his eyes, he motioned Mok to come near and without a word pointed straight ahead.

Mok nodded. He had spotted the anomaly at first glance and now seemed as fascinated as the hunter. Madame Ngha squatted beside the two men and stared intently without, however, being able to distinguish anything remarkable. Hoan, who remained standing, kept out of the way and appeared to dissociate himself from this charade. The two Jarai tribesmen exchanged a few words in low, almost inaudible voices, as if forced to whisper by some supernatural presence. Then Mok pointed for Madame Ngha.

'There!'

'I don't see anything strange,' she said in Jarai.

'There, there! That's not a plant.'

He advanced his finger until it almost touched a green stem, similar to the others on the bush. She started, exclaiming, 'Don't touch it!'

Trained more for scrutinizing reports than the vegetation of the jungle, her eye had not at first discerned any peculiarity. It took her a few moments to see that this particular stem was not exactly like the others, and that the tiny clusters of leaves at its tip were almost imperceptibly different from their neighbours. To the Jarai it was a glaring incongruity, but for her, as for any Vietnamese, it would have gone unnoticed.

However, if it took her a few moments to recognize the object of their agitation, her better disciplined brain set to work that much more rapidly. The sight of this stem triggered off an immediate chain of associations: the information contained in Thu's last report, the mysterious flights of the previous week.... In a fraction of a second she had grasped the connection between them.

Her reflexes were no less prompt. On a mere suspicion of the truth, and even before she had come to a conclusion, she realized instinctively the advantage to be gained from this chance discovery—provided, that is, certain precautions were taken. These she took at once, ruthlessly. As Hoan approached, intrigued by her behaviour, she rose and before he could so much as ask a question, clamped a lean, cool hand over his mouth, at the same time placing an imperative finger to her own lips, exacting absolute silence from everyone. She drew the three men away from the stem and only then, putting her mouth to the dumbfounded general's ear, did she whisper: 'Not a word.'

She addressed herself to the Jarai in the same way and asked Dju: 'Are you sure you can find this again?'

The hunter's silent laugh was a clear enough response. There was no chance of his going astray in the jungle. To be on the safe side, she asked him in gestures to mark the pathway back to the convoy. He understood at once, and without so much as a rustle of a blade of grass, the two tribesmen set out to obey. It was now obvious that for them the Vietnamese lady's every request was a direct order.

While they planted markers she returned with the general to what remained of the convoy. Only when they had reached the devastated area did she allow herself to say anything and give the general permission to do likewise. In a rather ill-tempered tone he demanded an explanation.

'Just a minute, please,' was her response. She scribbled a message in her notebook, tore out the page, and handed it to Van.

'Top secret. Transmit with extreme urgency.'

Then, turning back to Hoan: 'I have asked for Dr. Wang's assistance and told him enough to make sure he won't waste any time getting here. I know him: he'll be at your command post by this evening. You will please issue orders so he can be brought here even during the night. I'll be waiting for him.'

'Dr. Wang?'

'A Chinese scientist,' she said impatiently, 'a physicist who agreed to work with us and at the same time train our young students. He's one of the world's foremost electronics experts. You don't understand how this concerns him?'

In the face of his perplexity and more urgent matters now having been dealt with, she shrugged her shoulders, drew him a bit apart from the soldiers, and, after swearing him to secrecy, condescended to explain her behaviour. 'The object discovered by this hunter, General ... thank heaven for sending these hill tribesmen here! ... this object, this plant that isn't a plant, is one of our most terrible enemies, I'm almost certain it's an "ear of the jungle".'

'An ear of the jungle?'

'Our enemies call these little miracles "sensors", but one of my agents, unable to find a translation, has called them "ears of the jungle". I think we'll keep to that name: I find it expressive.'

As the general showed more and more bewilderment, she became increasingly animated, finally speaking with vehemence. 'The truth, General, the truth is that the jungle of the Annamite chain is now strewn, indeed riddled, with minute monitors: the slightest rumble of an engine in their vicinity is instantaneously transmitted to a central American base in Thailand; there the signals are immediately sorted and analysed by computers, and bombers are then directed to the transmitting area. Do you understand? That's how your convoy was located last night. It also explains the raid's miraculous precision.

'You've seen one of them, General, and could tell as well as I how deceptively like the surrounding vegetation it appeared, though thank heaven, not sufficiently to mislead a Jarai hunter. The Americans have used artists to make them look like the flora into which they'll be dropped. They embed themselves invisibly, deep in the environment. The camouflage is varied according to the region. Some, I know, will fall in the paddy fields on the plain: they will be disguised as rice shoots. I'm aware as well that a thorough study has also been made from this point of view on the flora of the high region. Our enemies think of everything. . . .'

'Remarkable ingenuity,' said the general, by now half-convinced.

'Admirable,' she acknowledged with an appreciative nod. 'They are both ingenious and powerful. But we'll be more cunning. We may not always have at our disposal the material means necessary for putting our ideas into practice, but this time. . . . Do you appreciate the possibilities offered by this discovery, especially if our enemies are not aware that we've made it? Now do you understand why I stopped you from saying anything?'

'I see. These ears can also pick up speech.'

'Any noise, as far as I know.'

'If that's the case, then maybe there's one near by listening in to our conversation at this very instant,' cried the general in alarm.

'Do you think I haven't thought of that? But don't worry, it's impossible. All the ground around here has been mangled and ploughed up by the explosions. No electronic device could have survived. The ears of the jungle perish once they've played their role. New ones will be dropped.'

'But the one discovered by the hunter must have been in good condition.'

'I certainly hope so, which is why I need Dr. Wang. They are equipped with an autodestructive device in case anyone imprudently touches them.'

'But the hill tribesmen were talking. They were even shouting. Didn't you tell me the hunter mentioned a foreign object several times?'

Madame Ngha smiled patronizingly.

'The Americans, General, no more understand Jarai than you do, and it hasn't occurred to them to get an interpreter. That I know, too.'

'Madame Ngha has an answer for everything,' conceded General Hoan with a bow.

8

Taking part of the escort, Hoan had gone off to help speed the specialist's journey. Madame Ngha entrusted Van with the task of finding her a sheltered spot where the mat, mosquito net, and rug that always accompanied her on her travels could be set up. As usual, that would suffice as her camp. She then came back towards the hill tribesmen, who were now all present. Mok asked permission to withdraw with his men, since too long an absence from the village might worry the women and, in any case, they ought to be getting back. The discussion about the three animals was just beginning again, but she cut it short by accepting the two pigs.

'The soldiers are going to prepare them and we'll be eating them this very day. But you must take the wild boar. ... And also,' she added on a sudden impulse that was not completely uncharacteristic, 'I want your women and children to eat their fill for a few days at least. Dju has rendered us a great service today, much greater than you can imagine.... There are still some undamaged sacks of rice in that overturned truck, and I'd like you to take as many as you can carry.'

The hill tribesmen cheered and Mok prostrated himself before her. It was a princely gift. Rice was even more cruelly lacking than venison in the village: a small handful was the daily ration.

After countless objections the chief thanked her effusively and had his men load up the sacks. Madame Ngha noticed with satisfaction that the Vietnamese soldiers spontaneously began helping them. She thanked the one who had set the example with a smile, for he had guessed what would please her. During this operation she reflected silently and, just as the Jarai prepared to take to the trail, again addressed Mok:

'Couldn't you send your hunters back to the village to reassure the women while you stay here and share our meal? We can eat the wild pig together, and it would please me if we could talk some more. I need you to teach me many things relating to the jungle, about which I know so little.'

The old man accepted with delight. 'But,' he added, 'if what you want to know concerns the jungle, you must speak to Dju. He knows it best and is one who will soon

41

succeed me as chief of the village, now that I am old.'

Proud of the invitation, Dju did not need to be pressed, and after renewed thanks to the Vietnamese woman, the column of hunters moved off with its precious burden.

'Let us eat,' said Madame Ngha. While the meal, which was to be served late, was being prepared she spent most of the day listening to the naïve accounts of her new friends, whom she had managed to put at ease. They told her in minute detail about their style of life, the upheaval brought into their peaceful existence by the war, and the legends they whispered in the village on moonlit nights. None of this was lost on her, but while her ear recorded these revelations and her memory stored away their essential points, available for instant retrieval should they be needed one day, she was deeply involved in pursuing her own preoccupations.

The conversation and her own thoughts had been disturbed only once, by an observation plane that flew over the ruins of the convoy several times, no doubt taking photographs to determine the seriousness of this blow struck against the enemy. The observers saw only wreckage, and nothing that might arouse their suspicions. At the first sound of its engine everyone had dispersed into the untouched part of the jungle, well away from the trail. The soldiers roasting the young pigs had located a sort of cave in the mountains where the fire could not be seen from the sky; there was still a little smoke, but it could easily be attributed to the remains of the blast. The airplane left after circling a few times.

'Let us eat!'

She sat on a flat stone between Mok and the hunter Dju. The soldiers followed suit, seating themselves around the three, their curiosity aroused as much by the unexpected contact with these pale-eyed men who hunted naked with arrows and spears as by the Vietnamese woman's manner and ease of expression in the natives' tongue. Everyone knew her by reputation, and those who had seen her before, taking pride in these former occasions, whispered legends about her. This was not the first time she had shared a meal with peasants and soldiers or chatted familiarly with them. Though she readily adopted an imperious tone with powerful generals—at times she was even severe with them—and was an exacting, occasionally tyrannical superior to her secretary, she knew how to put herself within reach of the common people and create a feeling of friendly camaraderie. She proved this now with the soldiers of the escort, the surviving drivers, and the two Jarai; improvising as hostess, she saw that each was served equitably, passed the plates herself, and jokingly upbraided Van, who in her opinion did not back her up quickly enough. She also acted as interpreter and translated the names of the dishes, at one moment into Vietnamese, the next into Jarai, to the great delight of the guests, who with shouts of laughter clumsily tried to repeat the unfamiliar syllables after her. All this was done without affectation and with great simplicity, though not for a moment did she interrupt her own chain of thought.

Only towards the end of the meal of wild pig, eaten with a little rice and served on broad leaves, did she turn over to Van the role of hostess, leaving herself free to approach with the hill tribesmen the subject that had been preoccupying her for hours.

'I would like to know whether the Jarai hunters, particularly Dju, whose eye is more piercing than an eagle's, could discern all the false stems like the one we saw today, if someone were to designate a specific and not too extensive area of the jungle.'

Mok smiled and turned towards Dju, who once again burst out laughing. It was his way of greeting an obvious truth.

'Not one could escape us,' he asserted. 'And all the hunters you've met, as well as those from the other Jarai villages, have eyes as sharp as mine. Especially now that we've seen one of them, we could make them out as easily as you

43

would notice a factory chimney among the tree trunks of the jungle.'

The neatness of this reply drew a smile of satisfaction from her.

'That's fine. And if I were the one who asked you to perform this small task in an area of the jungle I had selected, would you agree to do it? There would always be a little rice for your women and children.'

Consulting Dju first, Mok replied that it was possible. They now understood who their real friends were, and every hunter in the village would be put at her disposal, even if there was no rice, for Mok knew it was just as precious to the soldiers as the hill people.

'But,' he added, 'if this area of jungle is not within our territory, you will have to ask the help of hunters from another village. I think they'll agree when I've told them who you are ... particularly if Ami recommends it.'

'Ami?'

He did his best to explain who Ami was: a very wise old woman whose advice was sought by the Jarai on all serious matters.

'I'd be happy to meet her someday,' Madame Ngha mused.... 'I think it can be arranged. I'll contact you again soon. And if one of my friends comes on my behalf, he will give you this.'

She tore a bill in two, showing the half she was keeping and giving the other to Mok, who examined it carefully before stowing it away in his belt.

'All who come on your behalf will be well received.'

This agreement sealed, she abruptly changed the subject and asked in an indifferent tone: 'Didn't you tell me your whole village would have had enough meat for days if the bombs had fallen on that plain over there?'

'The Plain of a Hundred Thousand Buffalo? Yes, enough for days, perhaps even moons.'

'And if at a certain time the fire stones fell near a water hole I know,' Dju broke in, 'there would not only be enough game for us but for many of your soldiers, too. We would not be able to carry it all away.'

'And does Dju know of other areas in the jungle where here is as much game?'

'The Plain of a Hundred Thousand Buffalo is one of the best, but there are others almost as good. Dju knows them all; but the flying men are stupid and blind. They drop their stones anywhere. It is not the way to carry on a good hunt.'

She looked the Jarai straight in the eyes with unusual intensity, knowing that this conduct, considered impolite by the Vietnamese, was on the contrary highly appreciated by the hill tribes. Van, observing her chief at this moment, noticed her features relax into a sly smile and saw an odd glint appear in her eye. She recognized the most fleeting of her expressions and a feeling of curiosity made her quiver almost voluptuously, for she knew this smile and sudden glint meant that Madame Ngha was experiencing a lively intellectual satisfaction, provoked by the first glimmer of a subtle plot.

But the gleam was quickly gone. Nodding her head and speaking in a rather sententious tone, Madame Ngha simply echoed the Jarai hunter's remark. 'I definitely agree,' she said. 'Dju speaks with wisdom. Dropping stones at random! That is no way to have a fine hunt.'

2

CRICKETS

I

General Bishop arrived at the centre a little before eight o'clock in the evening, having eaten only his usual sandwich for dinner. He was set on being at his post just as darkness began to invade the Annamite chain, that moment when the Vietnamese convoys generally started out on their journey down the Ho Chi Minh Trail. Before proceeding to his own office he stopped by the monitoring room, again following a recently established habit; he appraised the room's impressive dimensions, glanced with curiosity and admiration at the enigmatic instruments that furnished it, and felt deeply proud at having been put in command of the army of minds animating it.

The room contained a mass of delicate and complex electronic instruments of a precision and sensitivity verging on the miraculous—the latest inventions of American genius in the field of secret strategic weaponry. They made it possible to hear and immediately locate any evidence of sound, in particular the faintest revving of engines on the Ho Chi Minh Trail, thanks to the sensors scattered throughout Vietnam and Laos—wherever the existence of a branch of that trail was suspected.

A large and expert staff worked in day and night shifts, listening to the live broadcast from the jungle. Each of its members had been put in charge of a well-defined sector. Equipped with headphones, he sat in front of a panel studded with dials, knobs, and switches allowing for adjustment and amplification, his mission to remain constantly on the alert and warn his superiors if any of the sounds picked up seemed to betray the passage of a convoy.

49

Colonel Shaw, scientific and technical aide to General Bishop, was seated at a central console. Helped by several assistants, he supervised the entire operation and made sure that its various objectives were carried out. Service S, installed in Thailand for three months now, was considered by the high command of exceptional importance for the conduct of the war and had already produced promising results. They expected it to force the enemy into abandoning the Ho Chi Minh Trail as a supply route for its troops operating in the south, thus affecting their capacity for prolonged resistance. The apparatus based on the sensors had been contrived by some of the most famous electronics specialists, and not without enthusiasm: the creation and perfecting of these little marvels was, for these scientific minds, a source of deep satisfaction. The conception, step-by-step realization, and installation in Thailand had been outlandishly expensive, but the anticipated results justified the allocation of lavish credit. The staff was composed of physicists, engineers, and technicians selected from among the most competent. They had been put into uniform and, according to their merits, allotted a few bars, in which they took little interest, Colonel Shaw least of all. The large monitoring room resembled some of the installations used by NASA to follow the flight paths of interplanetary rockets. The equipment employed in the service of the miniature detecting devices was considerable. The computers alone, the most important of which was an IBM S 360/65 enthroned in a neighbouring building, had cost a fortune.

Colonel Shaw stood up to meet the general.

'Any news, Shaw?'

'Everything's working marvellously, sir, but there's nothing suspicious for the moment.'

'The usual noises?'

'Just the natural sounds of the jungle at night, sir.'

Escorted by his assistant, General Bishop strolled slowly

around the room, frequently stopping at a table to put a question to the technician in charge. He enjoyed the personal contact with this new type of subordinate and treated them with more deference than if they had been real soldiers, ever curious and admiring when he saw them operating some mysterious control panel.

'What can you hear then? You look as if you're listening to a heavenly choir.'

This question had been addressed to a blue-eyed young man looking rather like a student, who seemed lost in a complacent dream, an ecstatic smile hovering on his lips. He put his earphones aside momentarily to reply.

'The cry of a night bird, sir. It's been going for about twenty minutes. I've heard it for several evenings now, but I just never seem to get tired of it. Sir, it's poetic. I read in a book that sometimes, when there's a moon, or simply on a clear night, it sings like that endlessly. I've looked it up: it's a kind of nightjar, but they sure don't sing like that back home.'

'Let's see,' said the general.

He leaned over and donned the headphones the other handed him, then gave a sign of appreciation. He could hear a series of rhythmic teeok, teeok, teeoks echoing at regular intervals. The young man was right, he thought; the song was suffused with a poetry that evoked moonlight. He felt himself overwhelmed by a gentle melancholy.

'Is the sound all right, sir?'

'I think so. But see for yourself.'

Shaw put the headphones on, listened for a few seconds, and frowned.

'There's a slight crackle we ought to be able to eliminate,' he said to the technician. 'Here. let me do it.'

He delicately manipulated some of the knobs on the panel, his eyes fixed on several dials whose needles shifted imperceptibly. Then his face cleared.

'Listen now, sir.'

Shaw could not tolerate the slightest imperfection in the adjustment of his equipment.

'It's perfect,' declared the general, who had taken delight in seeing this done.

'You could almost say the bird was in the room. A night-jar, you said?'

'A nightjar, sir, but of a particular species. I read that there are quite a few legends about it, but they weren't mentioned in my book.'

'I'll have to ask Thu,' murmured the general. 'She knows all the Vietnamese legends.... It's certainly a very strange cry: teeok, teeok....'

Then, the headphones clamped to his ears, he became silent, enraptured in turn. He would perhaps have stayed this way for some time, but he began to suspect that he had become the centre of everyone's attention. Sighing, he returned the apparatus to the young man and stiffened slightly.

'I see no harm in your thoughts taking a poetic turn, and it's fine to try and learn something about the area we have to keep under surveillance. But don't let this night bird distract you from what you know must still be your constant preoccupation: the detection of any evidence of human presence, especially the sound of those engines.'

The other assured him that he hadn't let his attention wander for a moment. The general passed on to the next and asked him a similar question. His face, on the contrary, was contorted as if he were in mortal agony, and he periodically wrung his hands with a nervous twitch.

'What's the matter?'

'Crickets, sir!'

'More crickets?'

'Yes, sir, damned crickets! They make an incredible racket. There's no other noise as hard on the nerves. At first, you can just manage to stand it. Some people even find it sort of musical; but in the long run it's like a Chinese torture. And they seem to be able to chirp like that for hours. One must have settled on the sensor this evening. It's awful, sir.'

52

'Let me see,' said the general again.

No sooner had he put the headphones to his ears than he winced. It wasn't his first experience with crickets, but he had to admit they were particularly virulent tonight. The sound he heard was so strident the whole room seemed to vibrate around him. At moments it was vaguely reminiscent of the howl of certain stringed instruments, though no orchestra could have rent the atmosphere in so barbarous a fashion. Every nerve in his body reverberated with it. He forced himself to keep the headphones on for a rather long while, then gave up and extricated himself with obvious relief.

'It certainly is very hard on the nerves, Shaw. We'll have to relieve the monitors more often when it's a matter of these crickets. They're intolerable.'

Colonel Shaw agreed and took note.

'You know, I'm well informed about crickets,' continued General Bishop, pleased at the opportunity to display his knowledge. 'Thu's told me some astonishing stories about these insects, and she knows them only too well. They abound in the region around Hue. Apparently, they're sometimes called cicadas there. But, whatever you call them, there are nights when they make an infernal row. If one of them gets into a house, which does happen occasionally so she says, there's no question of sleeping until it's been found and crushed. Are there many of them tonight?'

'A great many, sir. Even more than we've had on previous nights. A lot of the sensors are emitting the same cacophony. It's an unfortunate development.'

'But not surprising,' sighed the general. 'According to Thu, these insects tend to swarm in certain obscure parts of the high region.'

He proceeded with his rounds and interrogated another technician.

'Almost nothing tonight, sir,' he replied. 'I heard the plaintive cry of a water hen a few minutes ago, but she's

53

quiet now. Nothing else ... oh yes: the constant murmur of a stream, sir.'

Aside from the occasional revving of an engine betraying the passage of a convoy, this miracle of Western technology transmitted live into the air-conditioned room all the natural sounds of the jungle at night. Despite their perfection, the 'ears of the jungle' could hardly be asked to make a distinction between what was of interest to a military intelligence service and what might merely arouse one's poetic sensibility. Each night they faithfully transmitted the whole gamut, rich and infinitely diverse, of the indigenous nocturnal cries of the Annamite chain.

In the beginning it had been a surprise, and for the monitoring staff a rather delightful surprise. They had not anticipated it. Even Shaw had not thought of it, but he derived additional pride from this proof of the near perfection of his apparatus. Everyone—physicists, engineers, technicians, having spent their lives in universities, or laboratories and factories—felt stimulated by this nightly symphony, often letting their imaginations wander free in the depths of the mysterious tropical jungle, unknown to them and probably never to be known, but which science had brought within reach of their senses in this lost corner of Thailand, fitted up with all the modern conveniences to which they were accustomed.

General Bishop was the first to have been delighted with this unexpected aspect occasionally assumed by the espionage Service S was conducting here in Thailand. Initially he had decided that it relaxed the staff, helping them get more pleasantly through the hours that would otherwise have seemed interminable had they been spent in total silence under the earphones, and those poor unfortunates condemned to the inhuman torture of the crickets were obviously a special case. But he personally was so enthusiastic that he contemplated publishing a book after the war, the title of which he had already chosen: it would be *On Monitoring the Indochinese Jungle*. At night, when towards two or three o'clock he returned to his bungalow, before going to bed he took copious notes that had nothing to do with his military duties but were instead a commentary on the curious noises he had heard during the course of the evening. This work was for him the reward of a long vigil.

Thu, whom he had made his private secretary, had herself proposed typing these notes during her off-duty hours, for which he was especially grateful since he could hardly allow her to do it while on duty. He rewarded her by treating her particularly kindly, relaxing military discipline as much as possible and straining his imagination to make her assignment with Service S more comfortable.

In his office, where he spent part of the night, Shaw and his team had found it easy to install a loud-speaker, permitting him to hear all these interesting noises without having to use headphones. The order, of course, was to immediately submit to his judgment the slightest gasp of an engine or even the faintest metallic click that might signify a vehicle or armed troops. It was then up to him to take a military decision, which was in effect his sole function. But without these suspicious signs, often enough some of the jungle's natural echoes were relayed on the pretext that an intelligence officer could not neglect a single detail, however insignificant it might seem. Thus, General Bishop would often completely forget the war and, without leaving the armchair in which he sat several hundred miles from the mysterious universe where the Ho Chi Minh Trail unwound, sometimes allowed himself to be soothed by one of these strange symphonies, whose different voices became gradually familiar to him. The hollow hooting of the great horned owl was no newer to him than the cry of the nightjar; they had become too routine to justify disturbing him. That was done only on special occasions: the yapping of wild dogs in pursuit of prey, for example, or the belling of a herd of deer or the grunting of wild pigs foraging in the ground for roots.

55

There had been a few exceptionally choice moments, described by the general in his book with poetic enthusiasm. The trumpet call of an elephant, presumably awakened and overcome by the brilliant moonlight, followed by the sound of its feet pounding on the hard ground, which he had compared to the rumbling of thunder. Once he had heard, and it was the most precious piece in his collection, the distinct and prolonged snarl of a tiger stalking through the undergrowth. That particular night the general had unselfishly adjusted his loud-speaker to maximum volume and opened the door connecting his office with the monitoring room, enabling the entire staff, on lifting their headphones, to enjoy the programme.

Ears still buzzing with the chirp of the crickets, he entered his office, having advised Shaw, as he did each evening, to relay every noise that sounded suspicious or, failing that, any unusual animal cry. He sat down at his desk. In the opposite corner of the room was the place where Thu carried out her secretarial and occasional translating duties. General Bishop had decided to keep her near him and was quite satisfied with this arrangement. It was easier for the dictation of service memos, and apart from the pleasure he took in having the young Vietnamese woman's slender form and delicate, slightly childlike face before him, he had noticed that Thu knew and could identify all the noises of the jungle. She had acquired this knowledge while still a child, when she had travelled through the forests of the high region with her parents, who were then attached as servants to a family of Europeans. She never made a mistake in identifying the cry of each animal, or the song of each bird. The general could not have wished for a more valuable aide in the work he had undertaken.

'Thu will certainly be here before long,' he thought aloud, smiling.

She worked from nine till midnight. He insisted that she

did not stay any later, though she had frequently offered to work part of the night as he did. He already reproached himself for imposing these three extra hours of night work on her, but there were often urgent notes to be typed at that hour. But above all, perhaps, his office seemed empty and sad to him when she was not there. He tried to make up to Thu for this service by allowing her a great deal of freedom during the day.

He consulted his watch, established it was five minutes to nine, and concluded she would arrive any minute, punctual as always. Again he smiled fondly as he imagined her crossing his office, having greeted him with the regulation salute.

2

With regret Thu resigned herself to leaving the cold shower she had taken every evening before dinner ever since being allocated this bungalow. Dripping with water, she half opened the bathroom door and called: *'Thi Hai.'*

She was completely alone in the bungalow, but from the first day of her arrival here three months before, she had felt the need to people it. She waited a few moments, straining her ears to catch the sound of imaginary footsteps, then continued: 'Pass me my bathrobe.'

Her own hands took the bathrobe down from its hook and wrapped her in it caressingly, as all the while she continued the conversation, making the other responses necessary to the game herself.

'Has John finished eating?'

'He's finished, Madame.'

'You can go put him to bed. I'll dress myself and kiss him good night before I leave.'

* Vietnamese for housekeeper.

'Very well, Madame.'

'Wait a minute. How's little Thu?'

'I think she's better now, Madame. She no longer has a fever.'

'Let her go on sleeping in John's room, it's fresher than your quarters. The bed's perfectly big enough and it's more comfortable than your matting.'

'Very well, Madame. Thank you very much.'

Thu again listened carefully for the sound of receding footsteps, then her face contorted into a grimace that suddenly aged her. This pained contraction, a frequent expression of hers, was brought on whenever she felt her phantoms disappear, leaving her alone and distressed, or when a roar from the neighbouring base indicated that the B-52's were preparing to take off on another mission over Vietnam.

She went into her room and dressed quickly, putting on the uniform of the WACS. She permitted herself a single whim: a ribbon of white silk around her neck, the symbol of mourning. Her features tensed a bit more as she tied it; then she hastened into the living room, calling:

'Boy!'

'Madame.'

'You can set the table, but I'll only have a little soup and some fruit this evening.'

'Very well, Madame. I found some beautiful mangoes in the market.'

'Oh, thank you, I love them.'

The 'boy' was a phantom like Thi Hai, John, and little Thu. The 'boy' and the woman were husband and wife, parents of little Thu, who was only five or six years old.

Her face relaxed as she set out the requested dishes herself. These phantoms had existed before. Thu's parents had been in the service of two young English ethnologists, who between the two wars, the one with France and that with America, had stayed some time in Vietnam studying the tribes of the high country. Thu's father had served as their 'boy' and her mother as governess for young John, who was almost the same age as the little girl. Thu remembered this marvellous period and its journeys to the high plateaux with bitter nostalgia. The wife had taken a liking to her and helped her with her English, which she had been learning in a completely natural way while playing with John.

The second war had broken out. The English had gone home and her family returned to their village on the out-skirts of Hue. Thu had cried at leaving John, but then her need for affection had transferred itself to a younger brother, the second, who had been born a short time before and whom she cared for with maternal tenderness.

Madame Ngha's intuition had been correct. Thu could only live in a warm family atmosphere, which her game now recreated here. Time and time again she had tried to accomplish this after the crisis that had left her alone in the world: a B-52 bombardment that had pulverized her vil-lage, killing her parents and two brothers along with the dozens of other victims. But she had been unable to sur-round herself with these phantoms while among the Viet-cong commandos, in whose ranks she had enlisted. The jungle setting and the discomfort of the improvised encamp-ments had not lent themselves to it. Here, though, she suc-ceeded almost every evening.

Yet there had been a curious transposition of personalities in her game. In her conversations with these beloved ghosts she always played the role of the Englishwoman. Her parents had become her servants, and little Thu, an adorable child she had taken to immediately, she treated like her own son, John. This deviation of Thu's was achieved quite naturally from the very first day. Perhaps, living in this previously unknown comfort, which she now quite enjoyed, and finding herself mistress of a house with the right to air conditioning, an electric kitchen, and modern bathroom, she could not imagine the real Thu, the daughter of humble servants, in this role.

She drank her soup and ate two of the mangoes. After a cup of tea she cleared the dishes. Having no more need of the 'boy', she sent him away with a friendly word and went into her bedroom, now transformed into the children's room. She pulled the mosquito net aside and leaning over the bed kissed both John and little Thu. Then in a low voice she gave final instructions to Thi Hai, who stayed to keep watch over them while she was away. In the gentle tone she always used with her, she said: 'It doesn't bother you too much to stay up and keep an eye on them? I won't be back before midnight.'

With satisfaction she listened to Thi Hai's silent laughter, protesting she never went to bed before that hour. This had been one of her mother's habits. She insisted Thi Hai need not resume her duties before ten o'clock the next day, assuring her she could cope with little Thu herself. She also suggested she make herself some tea or coffee and, with a last glance towards the bed, withdrew on tiptoe, closing the door behind her without a sound.

She crossed the living room just as quietly, took a brief-case from the table, and was preparing to leave when she heard a discreet scratching at the door of the bungalow. She opened it and gave a start—her dream shattered. It was the gardener, and the gardener was certainly real enough.

He was Javanese and had lived in Thailand a long time. At the order of General Bishop, who loved flowers, he had recently been engaged by Service S and given the task of creating and maintaining little gardens in front of the staff bungalows. During the day he acquitted himself of these duties with taste and competence. At night he pursued other activities known only to Thu among all those in the monitoring centre.

He lifted the cap he always wore and held out a bouquet of flowers to the young woman.

'I thought that it is best to bring them in this evening, Miss,' he said in poor English. 'The messenger say it was urgent.'

'Well done, Sutan. Did he say anything else?'

'Only that everyone embraces you over there.'

'Thanks, Sutan. See you tomorrow.'

Sutan touched his cap and withdrew. Thu delved into the bouquet and drew out a capsule, which she opened. It contained a roll of paper. She unfolded it. It was Madame Ngha's last message.

She read it hastily, from time to time glancing at her watch. Happily it was not very long, and she rapidly assimilated the essential points. When she had finished she reread one passage attentively and a mischievous smile lit up her face, normally so tinged with melancholy.

3

'At last, Thu, there you are!'

The general's voice expressed relief far more than reproach, but Thu felt genuine remorse. She detested the possibility of anyone suspecting her of negligence.

'I'm terribly sorry, sir. My watch stopped. I'll stay later this evening.'

'Out of the question; you finish late enough as it is.'

The young woman's face betrayed such genuine sorrow at being five minutes late that the general was truly upset. For several minutes he did his best to persuade her it was unimportant. Meanwhile Thu had seated herself at her desk, opened her briefcase, and set to work.

'Anyway, there's nothing interesting this evening,' the general remarked. 'Crickets, just more and more crickets.'

'It's the time of year when their nightly concerts revive, sir.'

'Really? ... And there's also that night bird, the nightjar. Speaking of which, someone told me there are some legends....'

'There are many among the hill tribes. They call it the blacksmith bird.'

'The blacksmith bird? ... I see,' the general said with delight, 'that teeok, teeok, teeok is the sound of the hammer on the anvil.... But here I am preventing you from working.' (And what am I doing chatting on duty? he muttered to himself with a twinge of remorse.) 'Listen, Thu, you must tell me all about them, but not here; there's too much to do. Will you have lunch with me tomorrow?'

It wasn't the first time he had invited her to eat with him, and she always accepted gratefully. They had both plunged back into their work when there was a knock at the door and Colonel Shaw entered without even waiting to be asked in, which certainly indicated that something serious had happened.

'Engines, sir—truck engines. There are quite a few of them; it's a convoy for sure. You're being connected.'

Thu raised her head and listened attentively, an anxious expression on her face. The general pressed a button, and the sound was immediately transmitted into his office through the loud-speaker.

Engine noise; there was no doubt. A vehicle was labouring along a rough trail, with an occasional grinding of the gears. The general, his brow knit, listened to the variations in intensity as the truck approached an ear of the jungle, presumably passed close by, and then moved on, followed immediately by another. It was unmistakable: a convoy was threading its way along one of the Ho Chi Minh Trails.

'A whole string of sensors are transmitting the same thing in that sector, sir,' said the colonel. 'We've got them surrounded.'

Still Thu listened with the same worried expression, as if waiting for something. Suddenly her face relaxed and she stifled a sigh. A voice was heard singing in Vietnamese, accompanying the rumble of an engine.

'Do you understand that, Thu?'

'It's an old chant drivers sometimes hum to themselves to avoid falling asleep on long journeys.'

'There's no doubt about it,' decided the general. 'It's a convoy. I'll alert the F-4's.'

Once the ears of the jungle had played their role and the human brain, in this case General Bishop's, had weighed the situation and taken a decision, all that followed was a simple matter of mechanical routine.

On hearing the first suspicious signs, the general had already pushed the button that introduced the IBM S 360/65 into the circuit. It assimilated and analysed the transmitted information, singled out the convoy, and, without for a moment relinquishing it, calculated its speed, direction, length and number of vehicles, and, thanks to the profusion of jungle ears surrounding it, as Shaw had said, determined second by second the changing coordinates of its position.

General Bishop pressed two more buttons. One launched the F-4's, always ready to take off from a base in South Vietnam on this type of operation, and put them in direct contact with the IBM S 360/65. The other lit up a screen in his office on which appeared in large scale the region where the convoy was situated. On it twinkled several red dots representing the activated ears of the jungle. The convoy itself appeared as a thin blue ribbon moving slowly through the network of red lights.

'A little electronic miracle,' remarked Shaw, his usual comment at moments like this.

The general agreed solemnly. He too was impressed by this masterpiece of technology, especially since he understood nothing about how it worked. There were nights when he was tempted to consider his assistant a wizard.

His task now finished, the general had nothing more to do than wait for the results of the operation, which within twenty minutes of the launching of the raid were signalled simultaneously over the loud-speaker and on the big screen. The heavy panting of the engines was abruptly smothered by the exploding of the first bombs. The roar lasted only a second, then gave way to absolute silence. At the same time the red dots and the blue ribbon of the convoy disappeared from the screen. The operation was over. The F-4's had played their role, a modest one, on the whole. The jungle ears were out of commission; others would be dropped the next night. The convoy must have been severely hit, if not utterly destroyed.

'Where did that happen?' General Bishop asked indifferently.

Shaw had no idea. He had never even looked at a map of the region. The general glanced briefly at the coordinates of the area indicated on the screen, then leafed through a set of ordnance maps, trying to get his bearings.

'It's near the junction of Vietnam, Cambodia, and Laos,' he said, 'a sort of plateau in an extremely rugged, mountainous region. . . . The jungle is shown as very dense there. There are no paths, assuming the map is correct, and the approaches are steep. Funny idea to take trucks through there, don't you think, Thu?'

There were times when General Bishop felt the need to transcend the mechanical universe in which he found himself immersed and discuss the human side of these operations. Failing Shaw, to whom it was obviously impossible to admit even the existence of a human side, he turned to his secretary, whose judgment he greatly appreciated. She promptly replied: 'It seems strange indeed, sir. But they probably imagined they'd deceive us by taking an absurd route. They never thought it would occur to us to bomb this scrubland.'

'That must be it, Thu. But there they were mistaken. We now have ears everywhere.'

He again leaned over his ordnance map and grumbled.

'These maps are very badly done. There's a name here, but I can't even read it. Would you have a try, Thu? You've got better eyes than me.'

'The letters are really small, sir ... still, yes, that's it ... the Plain of a Hundred Thousand Buffalo, sir.'

'The Plain of a Hundred Thousand Buffalo? Odd name ... picturesque, anyway.'

'I know that area very well, sir,' said Thu with a smile of amusement. 'I've stayed there before with my parents. It's the hill tribesmen who named it the Plain of a Hundred Thousand Buffalo; I seem to remember its being very well stocked with game—so I suppose that's why.'

A telephone rang. The general picked up the receiver, exchanged a few words with someone, and replaced it.

'Confirmation of the raid,' he said briefly. 'A success apparently. Quite a few blazes. Another convoy won't reach the south intact. That'll teach them to use the Plain of a Hundred Thousand Buffalo.'

Colonel Shaw had left them to return to his post in the monitoring room. The general dipped into his papers for a moment, then checked the time.

'Thu, it's late and I don't really need you any more. Go and get some sleep,' he said.

She protested that she wasn't tired, but with paternal authority he insisted.

'And don't forget we're lunching together tomorrow. You can tell me some of the legends about the blacksmith bird.'

She obeyed and left the room after arranging her things, finding her way back to the bungalow in the dark. There, taking care not to awaken John and little Thu, she acquainted Thi Hai in a confidential tone with the amusing new game dreamed up by her dear Aunt Ngha.

Alone, the general tried to absorb himself in the compilation of a report destined for General Headquarters. But his mind was elsewhere. He stood up and took a few steps around his office, then stretched and sat down again, murmuring in a low voice: 'After all, I've done a good night's work. That should deserve a little relaxation.'

He hesitated again, then made up his mind and called Shaw on the intercom.

'Put through some jungle sounds, Shaw,' he said rather like a schoolboy caught in the act, '... I'm just not up to it tonight; I need something to wake me up.... Yes, even if there's nothing new.... No, not crickets, obviously! Hold on, the blacksmith bird, maybe.... What? Yes, sure, the nightjar, the teeok teeok teeoker! I could use it tonight; I'm fed up.'

4

The whole affair had been organized by a master, with a perfection and solicitude for detail in which one could recognize the hand of Madame Ngha. She had, in fact, wanted to supervise all the preparations for the operation herself, which she saw as the first of a long series entailing two distinct phases, one to take place on the Plain of a Hundred Thousand Buffalo, the other about thirty miles from there in a region more easily accessible to trucks.

Some of these preparations had required finesse; and though the first tape recordings had not presented any particular difficulties, she had none the less been determined to be there along with Dr. Wang. It had all taken place in an isolated part of North Vietnam, where enemy aircraft only rarely penetrated. The essential piece of equipment, an ordinary tape recorder, had been placed at the edge of a trail roughly laid out in the forest, and trucks, one following a slight distance behind the other, directed to file past. The path had been strewn with obstacles: potholes, rocks, roots, similar in every way to those met with by the real convoys in their journeys towards the south. The drivers, long accustomed to the Ho Chi Minh Trail, had been chosen for their experience, reliability, and discretion. One of them was Nam, who had not been terribly surprised at the instructions they had received: to drive exactly as they did normally, and not hesitate to race the engine, grind the gears, or squeal the brakes whenever necessary. The operation had naturally occurred at night. Nam had followed these instructions to the letter and, though not understanding the implications of the exercise, had been convinced it was more than just a game. When Madame Ngha had asked him to hum the popular chant (a signal to reassure Thu) he did so with a smile, knowing the Vietnamese lady always had her head on her shoulders, even when it seemed otherwise.

Only six trucks had been used. They made themselves heard by passing single file in front of the recording apparatus, then describing a large circle and returning to file past it again. A subsequent editing of the tape had eliminated the silences. After several attempts that only half satisfied them, Madame Ngha and Dr. Wang had finally judged the illusion perfect: the sound was exactly like that of a long, continuous convoy forcing its way along a difficult mountain trail. A large number of such tapes had been prepared.

Recording the crickets had been more troublesome and demanded more numerous attempts. Not that these insects were difficult to come by. On the contrary, Thu had not been lying when she declared that certain regions of Vietnam were infested with them. A sufficient quantity had soon been gathered after promising the village urchins a reward. The awkward problem lay in making them chirp at the right moment while still keeping them close enough to the tape recorder, for they would only chirp at certain hours of the night and then only when they felt themselves at liberty. It had required patience and the devising of little grass cages, which prevented them from escaping without giving the impression of captivity. But the difficulties had only finally been overcome when an intelligence officer had the fortunate idea of artificially stimulating their concert by having a musical instrument played, a sort of crude violin made at his request by a peasant. It had imitated the noise of the insects, and though not well enough to replace them (Madame Ngha had been determined there should not be a single false note in her scenario), enough to initiate their strident chirping. When a suitable number of these tapes had been recorded, Madame Ngha had set to work having the terrain prepared.

In this the Jarai, tempted by the promise of a reward and wanting above all to render her a service, had been of invaluable assistance. She had first had them rake, as if with a fine-tooth comb, a section of trail in a particularly dangerous area through which she had decided an important convoy was to pass. Here they had found a veritable plantation of jungle ears, detecting more than a hundred in the zone to which she had limited the search. It had only been twenty-five yards wide and about eighteen miles long, since covering a greater area would have demanded too much work and was in any case unnecessary for her plan. Once Mok had assured her that no more existed in this zone, a tape recorder with automatic release and armed with a tape emitting the chirping of crickets had been placed at the base of each device, in this way staking out the entire dangerous part of the route.

She had thought for a long time before adopting this tactic. It would have been easier, as Van had suggested, to simply have the jungle ears removed. Dr. Wang had studied them at length, and despite their autodestructive system he and his assistants now knew how to handle them without causing damage. But she had feared that an absolute silence in a region the enemy had taken the trouble to put under surveillance with such a wanton number of devices might raise the alarm, and also that, regardless of Mok's assurances, some of them close enough to the trail to betray the noise of a convoy might have escaped the eyes of the hill tribesmen. The crickets had eliminated both these drawbacks by drowning out every other sound in the dangerous zone. Leaving nothing to chance, however, she had made sure of this by faithfully reproducing the prepared sector in North Vietnam, and calling for a rehearsal. The results had been conclusive.

When the real route had been marked out, she had a strip of land on the Plain of a Hundred Thousand Buffalo investigated in the same fashion. It was near the water hole where tracks had revealed to Dju the fact that the herds went there to refresh themselves at an hour of the night he was now able to determine exactly.

They had discovered only a dozen ears of the jungle there, quite enough for her plan. They were moved through the courtesy of the Chinese specialist and cunningly placed to attract the bombs onto the point most propitious for a fruitful hunt. At their feet were the appropriate recordings, those revealing the passage of a convoy.

That should have been sufficient preparation for a single operation, but Madame Ngha had no intention of leaving it at that and had taken into account the observation planes that might risk exposing the deception after the strike. She had brought to the site of this remote-controlled raid some of those remnants the enemy would expect to find on his photos: the wreckage of trucks. Found almost everywhere along certain parts of the trail, it was transported on the backs of men or on bicycles or improvised carts, silent vehicles drawn by the soldiers. They had been threatened with severe punishment if they so much as uttered a single word. This precaution was unnecessary, however. Like Nam they had guessed, without even being acquainted with all the details of operation, that it had something to do with a clever trick, and their Asiatic love of subtlety led them to throw themselves wholeheartedly into ensuring its ultimate success.

With a sigh, for fuel was as precious as ammunition, Madame Ngha had sacrificed several drums of gasoline and fuel oil, which would serve to create suitable explosions and fire.

Nothing remained to be done but adjust the release mechanisms of the tape recorders to the hour Dju had indicated. This had again been an easy enough task for Dr. Wang and his team. At last they had stealthily withdrawn, leaving this corner of the savage jungle to regain its normal tranquillity and allow the herds of buffalo, once they felt reassured, to gradually return.

This double operation achieved a double success, fully justifying the scrupulous care devoted to it and the congratulations Uncle Ho himself afterwards expressed to those who had secretly participated, not forgetting his dear niece Thu. She confirmed in a subsequent report that no one had suspected the ruse.

The F-4's, in obedience to the computers on board, which were themselves directed by the IBM S 360/65, had released their bombs at the desired moment over the exact point to which the ears of the jungle had summoned them, covering a radius extensive enough to leave a good haul for those who waited in the dark a reasonable distance away.

The results had been verified at daybreak by a patrol of hill tribesmen and Vietnamese soldiers. Two herds of wild buffalo had been decimated, and about forty of the finest beasts now lay on the ground along with a profusion of smaller game: roebuck, mountain hares, wild peacocks, wood pigeons, and jungle cocks, which had been pierced by flying splinters or knocked senseless by the explosions.

According to the instructions given by Madame Ngha, this haul was to be divided into two equal parts, but this time Mok held his own in the polite discussions engaged in on the subject and emerged the victor. He wanted to carry off only ten buffalo and some of the smaller game, which were enough to fill all the jars in the village and to feast on for many moons. The Vietnamese's share, after being cut up, was immediately transported to an underground centre of the Ho Chi Minh complex, where a team was waiting to prepare and preserve it. This venison was highly appreciated by General Hoan's commissariat, which sometimes came up against insurmountable difficulties in this region. Everyone hoped the operation would be repeated at more or less regular intervals, which later happened, and though their luck varied, there was often an appreciable catch. In this way the American air raids succeeded in providing a partial solution to the problem of provisioning the thousands of men who toiled along the Ho Chi Minh Trail.

On that same morning Madame Ngha had decided to go to a different centre, the terminus of another sector of the trail, where the real convoy was due to arrive at daybreak. This second part of the operation was also an unequivocal success. The column of trucks arrived safely, missing neither a vehicle, sack of rice, nor case of munitions. This convoy, an important one, had even reached the stopover point a little sooner than expected, having been able to move slightly faster than usual.

This was due to the crickets. Nam, now head of the column on this section of the trail, had been informed of these acoustic markers and been begged not to deviate from them. He quickly perceived that they made his task much easier, the crickets' concert composing a sustained ensemble of easily followed cues. So he had stepped up the pace a little, gaily directing the accompanying convoy as if to the strains of a triumphal march played by an orchestra of strident violins.

This morning, as she celebrated their twin successes, Madame Ngha was already devising similar operations in her head. She feared too great a proliferation of crickets might eventually arouse the enemy's suspicions. Thus, in order to vary the sound effects, she intended to have specialists carry out a study of all the noises possible in the jungle at night.

But her chief fear was that the monitoring service might finally notice that the chirping of the crickets formed a continuous line, in an approximate north-south direction, along the Annamite chain. On this point, though, her fears were

71

groundless, as Thu later reassured her: whenever it was a question of crickets, General Bishop neglected to transmit the data to the IBM, and the coordinates of these transmitting points consequently remained unknown.

3
NAPALM

I

Ami took a puff on the pipe she had just lit and in a sponta-
neous gesture of friendship presented it to Madame Ngha,
who was seated at her side. She thanked her gravely and
took two long puffs in turn, appearing to appreciate the
taste of the acrid tobacco. The conversation, till then general
and rather trivial, gave way to a more serious exchange
between the two women.

'It is not the hill tribesmen's fault if for some time the
hunts have been less fruitful,' said Ami.

'I know. It's the fault of our enemies, who are now using
new weapons.'

A fraternal banquet had concluded the little festivity to
which the Jarai hunters had been invited. It took place in
broad daylight, near a position providing safe natural shelter
in deep caves penetrating a mountainside, able to serve as
refuge in the event of an air raid and through which the
cooking smoke could be conducted by long subterranean
passages towards another, distant slope. There had been no
alert that day, and nothing had disturbed the programme of
celebrations, with songs, rounds, and a long performance
given by a travelling theatrical troupe succeeding one another in an atmosphere of simplicity and gaiety.

These performances were not uncommon on the trail.
Uncle Ho encouraged the arts and urged the best actors to
organize shows for the soldiers as often as possible. This
they made a point of honour, at times playing in the hottest

75

theatres of the war, thus sustaining the soldiers' morale as well as their political faith. Indeed, the plays put on always included allusions to the political situation and the struggle, simple allusions within everyone's grasp and often humorous, though always tending to serve the cause of the young Republic.

There had been a certain opulence to the festivities that day. Madame Ngha had wanted to celebrate the alliance with her new friends the Jarai properly. She had likewise preferred not to preside officially, but to participate in an active manner, pursuing her usual habits of poking into things and mixing with people whenever possible.

She was inclined to be present for another reason. Ami had come, and she wished to meet her as much as Ami desired to make her own acquaintance. She had sat among the hill tribesmen throughout the performance, occasionally translating phrases for them when the mimicry of the actors was not sufficient to explain the plot, though that was rare. The people of the high country seemed to enjoy themselves every bit as much as the Vietnamese soldiers, and both punctuated the repartee with resounding laughter.

An especially well-prepared meal had followed the play. Van, who was capable of fulfilling the most diverse functions, had, at her boss's request, supervised the preparations and sent for a group of young girls skilled in the art of making *naymes* and other special Vietnamese delicacies. A feast of this quality was practically unheard of on the trail, but Madame Ngha had provided the necessary funds. Seated beside Ami, she took care to maintain the gay and friendly atmosphere and succeeded marvellously. The other guests— the Jarai hunters, the soldiers undistinguished by rank, and the convoy drivers—mingled, chatting cheerfully together. By now Vietnamese and tribesmen were beginning to understand one another better, having learned a few words of each other's language, though at times rather oddly resorting to the vestiges of French some of them had retained. Only the escort, still armed yet almost invisible, had remained aloof, discreetly allowing the guests to forget the war that hovered constantly over the jungle. At the end of the meal the Jarai had lit their pipe, and passed it now and then to the soldiers. Ami offered hers to Madame Ngha, who appeared deeply touched by this attentiveness.

'It's our enemy's fault. They've modified their tactics,' repeated Madame Ngha. 'They no longer drop many conventional bombs, but napalm instead.'

'Napalm?'

Madame Ngha explained that the use of this substance or phosphorus resulted in an intense heat that consumed all the vegetation, permitting the flying men easy observation of the areas they thought to be dangerous.

'That is what the hunters reported to me,' said Ami, nodding her head. 'But along with the foliage and plants, this napalm ...'

She had remembered the word perfectly, and it was clear she would never forget it. Since her arrival she had uttered only a few remarks, content with observing and listening to her hostess and, as was only proper between courteous people, waiting until the end of the meal to touch on more serious topics. In this respect the instincts of the Jarai placed them on a level with the most sophisticated Asiatics and Westerners.

The hunters of the village had presented her with so extraordinary a portrait of this lady of Vietnam that she had been determined to accept the invitation, despite her advanced age and the great distance to be travelled through the jungle. The hill tribesmen had taken it in turn to carry her in a kind of bamboo sedan chair.

As for Madame Ngha, she had divined Ami's importance and spared no effort to be agreeable to her, knowing how to be charming when she judged it useful. For some time she had been consumed by the desire to form a personal opinion of this old Jarai woman, who was regarded almost as a queen by her tribe. But to do this she had no need to stare

77

incessantly, as the other did at her. Two or three remarks and a simple glance were enough for her to evaluate Ami and understand why the Jarai always sought her counsel. Well before they began puffing on the pipe, it was evident that the two women had come to appreciate each other's worth.

Ami was the first to approach the immediate problem. As she had mentioned, the latest hunting expeditions had been disappointing, and the hunters had returned empty-handed. Their only consolation lay in conjuring up the brilliant successes of previous moons.

'Along with the foliage of the trees and plants, this napalm consumes the flesh of the slaughtered animals and makes it inedible. The hunters find nothing but carcasses transformed into flakes of charcoal.'

'Yes. I know about that. It makes our hunt an unforgivable waste. I think we too will have to modify our tactics, and try to have this napalm diverted onto places where there's little game. What does Ami think about it?'

'Ami thinks the hunters were right. The lady from Vietnam possesses both intelligence and power.'

'The power is in the hands of our great chief.'

'I have heard speak of him.'

'I do my best to help him.'

'We will also do everything possible. We have now understood who our real friends are. . . . Speaking of which, I want to tell you that for some time now we have modified our prayer for averting war.'

Here again, the instincts of the hill people made her adopt the manner of the most refined of Asiatics, who consider themselves peasants if they leap directly to the point and fail to punctuate the conversation with digressions, usually of a character flattering to the listener. Madame Ngha, with subtle Chinese blood in her veins, could hardly take exception to this display of courtesy. On the contrary, she encouraged Ami to continue.

'For moons and moons our prayer for averting war has begun:

Oh Master, Lord of Fire. We who are here are trapped, crushed by the Vietnamese, by the Cambodians....'

She stopped to observe Madame Ngha, who without batting an eyelash said simply: 'I like the Jarai prayers very much. Would Ami care to recite all of it?'

The old woman bowed and continued:

'We who are here can no longer dig, or cultivate the fields, or plant the rice, or pull the weeds. We who are here have suffered many deaths, seen many corpses, all from the battles. We who are here count on your aid and prostrate ourselves....'

She recited the entire prayer, which ended with the words:

'Make our enemies die, those who are wicked to our people, make them die this very moment.

'That is how the prayer used to go. But now, as I said, in each of the villages we have changed the first words, and replaced Vietnamese with flying men.'

Madame Ngha suddenly felt her body suffused by a warm glow, and her eyes shone with proud satisfaction. These words marked the success of her policy. Ami was silent for a moment; then, this essential digression over, she returned to the immediate problem: 'You said you would try to have this napalm diverted to regions poor in game. As I answered, we will do our best to help you carry out that plan. Our hunters know of mountains where there are almost no animals and where the napalm would consequently do little damage.'

'I thank you.'

Ami then fell silent and seemed to concentrate on the bowl of her pipe as it hissed and sputtered. At last she resumed: 'Before, these were the regions we chose for cultivating our mountain rice. Otherwise, of course, the deer and buffalo would quickly have ruined our harvests.'

She had said this in an indifferent tone; too indifferent, Madame Ngha promptly decided. Age had not dimmed the clarity and penetration of Ami's eyes, which had taken on a singular brilliance, out of all proportion to the blandness of her remark. The Vietnamese woman, able to analyse the minutest details of character, was certain this observation was not made by chance. She did not give any indication of this, however, but simply encouraged Ami to continue, adopting the same polite, banal tone herself.

'Rice,' she said, 'you must often lack rice. It's not possible to live only on the flesh of animals.'

'No, it is not. Rice is essential. And the meagre *rays** we have planted around the village no longer yield anything. The soil is no good. It is completely dead now. We must change their location, as we used to do every two or three years. With this war going on it is not easy.'

Another silence, again broken by Madame Ngha.

'Perhaps I could provide seeds.'

'Thank you, but it is not that. We could get enough by ourselves. No, the real difficulty ...'

A final silence. Then she leaned forward and spoke more forcefully. Madame Ngha realized she had at last come to the point.

'The great difficulty,' said Ami, 'is the burning. To plant our mountain rice we first have to burn a place for it in the jungle.'

* Mountain rice fields planted by the Jarai after burning back the jungle.

2

This time Madame Ngha's feelings were expressed by a slight flutter of the eyelashes, a reaction feebly disproportionate to the sudden, dazzling intellectual exultation that had sprung from the pleasure and respect she felt as she finally realized what the old woman was driving at.

The two women were now alone, chatting in private, while around them the soldiers removed the pots containing the remnants of the meal. The Jarai smoked in silence. After taking a leisurely look around, Madame Ngha calmly responded.

'I see. Before planting the paddy you have to burn the jungle and destroy undesirable vegetation, so that the light can get to the soil ... and I suppose burning the jungle isn't easy at the moment.'

'Right,' agreed Ami, pleased her hint had been taken.

'It must be difficult for several reasons. First, your fire would attract the flying men, and then, it's not really the right season, is it? The rains have already fallen. The forest is damp and the fire wouldn't exactly spread by itself.'

'Not by itself, that is it exactly,' Ami agreed once again.

'So to create a blaze you would have to sprinkle the undergrowth with ... gasoline, for example.'

'That is how we did it before. But we cannot get hold of it any longer.'

'Gasoline ... or maybe even napalm, no?' asked Madame Ngha with a delicious smile.

For the first time since the beginning of the festival Ami smiled too.

'The lady from Vietnam is even shrewder than the hunters

thought,' she said. 'She has guessed my plan. She already knows the authorization I wish to ask of her.'

'Ami doesn't need authorization. The jungle belongs to everyone, and above all to the Jarai who inhabit it.'

'But I prefer to have your permission. Your soldiers might be astonished to see our men prowling around at night in the areas burnt by the napalm.'

'So if I have understood correctly, your idea is to use these burnt tracts for sowing. In that way a part of your work will have been done for you.'

'And the most difficult part. That is exactly it. Our men have already located several favourable tracts. The ground is cleared of vegetation, and much better than we could have done in the past. The ashes fertilize the soil. The rice just begs to grow there. The manioc too.'

Madame Ngha mentally examined every aspect of this plan, the spirit of which coincided remarkably well with some of her own ideas, and agreed with the philosophy of war she had acquired. Still, with a preoccupied air she raised some objections.

'The flying men will see the rice growing. They have eyes and powerful glasses for extending their vision. They'll think it is we who are making use of the cleared ground and return with their machines to destroy you.'

'They will see grass. That always grows after a burning if it is not pulled up. But they will not know it is rice. They will think it is just natural vegetation, on the condition . . .'

'On what condition?'

'On the condition that we take care to sow it irregularly, and not in straight lines like your peasants on the plains do. We would also intersperse it with manioc, which looks wild. And there must be a thousand other ways to deceive them. We shall have to think about it.'

'Ami can rest assured my soldiers won't disturb this plan in any way,' cried Madame Ngha with rare animation. 'Now I realize that Ami's mind is even subtler than my own. I'd never have thought of that myself.'

The old woman demurred, nodding her head.

'The spirits sometimes inspire me,' she said modestly. 'And sitting up there in my hut, I have nothing else to do but think.'

'I'd never have had that idea,' insisted the Vietnamese woman. 'I thank you a thousand times, for we are going to carry out this plan, too, but on other parts of the trail where we won't be in your way. Rice is scarce for us as well. To provision our troops in the south we've been obliged to transport it, and that's very costly.'

'The jungle is vast, and the trails your soldiers follow long and numerous. Now that they have started, the flying men will create arable surfaces everywhere. Though the *rays* will be small and the yield probably meagre, there will be thousands of them, enough to feed your people and mine. All thanks to napalm.'

The festival was over and the serious business settled to everyone's satisfaction. Ami and the Jarai took the path back to their village, where they would prepare sacrifices and recite prayers to the spirit of the earth, that he might grant them abundant harvests. Madame Ngha, her brain overstimulated by their conversation, remained thoughtful a while, devising a grandiose scheme she intended to submit to the President the very next day.

As this project matured, she and her small escort reached the spot in the jungle where a vehicle waited to take her back to North Vietnam. She took the rather uncomfortable seat in the rear and gave the signal to depart. Van, who had followed, placed the briefcase at her side. Madame Ngha never wasted her time and, ignoring the rough jolts of the trail, always took advantage of these journeys. If she was not pondering, eyes half-closed, she would acquaint herself with a report, reread an important document, or write a memo.

Today it so happened that her deliberations on the current project were finished and all the details fixed in her mind; they were so simple she did not even feel the need to make a note of them. A conversation with Uncle Ho would be enough to put the plan into effect. Nor were there urgent documents to consult. She was delighted. It would permit her to relax for a few hours.

However, Madame Ngha never devoted the leisure hours she sometimes allowed herself during the day to sleep or complete rest. For her, relaxation simply meant a change of occupation, and among those that distracted her without being a waste of time, reading was her favourite: reading often considered frivolous by her compatriots, especially the novels and essays by American authors she felt her position did not permit her to ignore.

This she did today. Thanks to the solicitude of her secretary, who knew her tastes, there were always several books she thought her boss might find interesting stuffed in the heavy briefcase. Madame Ngha took them out, looked at the titles, and skimmed over the editor's comments, then replaced the pile, keeping only one book that, eyes bright with curiosity, she began to read.

It absorbed her for the entire journey, which lasted the rest of the day and most of the night, until her travelling companions and worries were forgotten. She broke off only rarely: once, as dusk began to darken the trail, to get a miniature pocket light from her bag, which she used to sweep the pages line by line; at other times, to underline a passage in pencil or make a brief comment in the margin. She always brought the same scrupulous attention to these books as she did to her service documents, ever anxious to learn some new element of the enemy's psychology. She had thus devoured and annotated the report of the Warren Commission, the Kinsey report, *The Peter Principle*, and many other works. What completely monopolized her attention during this journey was an essay dealing with the enslavement of women, in particular American women: it was *The Feminine Mystique*, by Betty Friedan.

Van, with nothing to do but observe her boss, saw a curious

84

smile appear repeatedly on her lips. Although she was in no way a fool—or she would never have been chosen as Madame Ngha's secretary—she could not prevent herself from smiling as well. Distracted for a moment, Madame Ngha noticed this and, feeling in a good mood, smiled more broadly, exchanging with Van a look full of complicity as she did so.

So in this cheerful atmosphere the vehicle, packed in front with soldiers, crossed over the passes and finally, reaching a better road, sped on towards the north, leaving far behind the high country, its primitive tribes, and the Ho Chi Minh Trail.

3

Uncle Ho gave his approval without any difficulty. The ingenuity and obvious advantages of the plan had captured his imagination, and with enthusiasm he promptly ordered it put into practice on a vast scale throughout Vietnam.

So it was that amidst the countless paths of the Ho Chi Minh Trail, to points selected in advance and carefully avoided by the convoys, the skilful sound effects transmitted by the ears of the jungle attracted the enemy aircraft like moths to a flame. The phosphorus and napalm started fires almost everywhere, carving out innumerable gaps in the tropical forest through which darted the sun's benevolent rays, enriching the soil now covered with a layer of ash, that irreplaceable fertilizer. These new *rays*, of a variety unforeseen by any agricultural engineer, were tilled at night in preparation for the future harvests. The Vietnamese sowed a multitude of fields from north to south, along the entire length of the Annamite chain. The Jarai were content with only a few, located a reasonable distance from their villages and extensive enough to satisfy their modest needs. Before the seeding, also carried out at night, they sacrificed a pig and a jar of rice wine while reciting the prayer that began:

'Oh Spirit of the Earth, we summon you here, O Earth Spirit, to drink rice wine and eat liver of pig. Be beneficent, Spirit of the Earth. Give us in abundance the coolness, the rice....'*

Then, Mok having seen a river in a dream the following night, they knew the spirit of the earth had authorized the sowing of the new *rays*. And so it was done, and successfully. Ami, before Madame Ngha's departure, acquainted her with her point of view on all this, that it was good to seek the favour of the spirits with offerings and prayers, but neither was there anything wrong in aiding their task with patient, solitary meditation.

Such a remark could hardly fail to arouse echoes in the mind of the Vietnamese woman, and she reproached herself for not having been lucid enough when confronted with the over-all problem of the bombings. She herself began to follow the advice of the old tribeswoman, thinking more clearly about the problem and encouraging her collaborators to do likewise.

The fruits of these contemplations were soon to be seen in other practical applications, and not only in the high country, but on the plains, where there was no protection from the bombings. The impulse given by Madame Ngha gradually filtered through all the layers of the population, and the peasants and soldiers vied with one another to come up with the most ingenious discoveries. It was from this period on that, throughout Vietnam, from north to south, the slogan was whispered: Transform bad into good. It was then that carp and other fish were seen to prosper in the craters blasted out by the huge bombs. It was then, too, that

* *Jarai Prayers.*

in different regions other hollows were put to use and transformed into reservoirs to solve the problem of irrigation, which until that time it had never been possible to do satisfactorily.

A dedicated rivalry seized everyone, not the least enthusiastic being the small group of specialists responsible for handling the ears of the jungle. The Chinese soul of Dr. Wang could hardly fail to respond delightedly to this stratagem, and he made it a point of honour to place flawless equipment at Madame Ngha's disposal, whose genius he had recognized. Ranking among the world's most illustrious scientists, he had abandoned his work in advanced theoretical physics to devote himself with a few of his assistants to the quest for more and more convincing and subtle recordings, capable of attracting the enemy bombers to any specified point at the desired hour, while another group of his collaborators specialized in elaborating varied sound effects derived from the jungle and suitable for camouflaging the nightly passage of convoys on the Ho Chi Minh Trail.

In the bungalow Thu occupied in Thailand these Asiatic subtleties took the singular form of an idealized game, frequently enlivening it with childish laughter. As Thu left the bathroom she called to the housekeeper: 'Thi Hai, did you say the children had been good today?'

'Very good, Madame.'

'Then they must have a reward. We're all going to play a game together. You can put them to bed a little later.'

'Very well, Madame.'

Thu pricked up her ears and heard a tumult of joyful shouts coming from her room, followed by the patter of bare feet on the floor. She opened her arms so that John and little Thu, already in their pyjamas, could tumble into them.

'You're going to be General Bishop,' she said to John. 'I'll be our Aunt Ngha, and Thi Hai, you're playing too. You can be my secretary, Van.'

'I wouldn't know how, Madame,' protested the house-keeper, laughing.

'It's easy. All you have to do is to put on my large sun-glasses.'

'And me?' asked little Thu.

'I've saved the role that's the most fun for you. You're going to be an ear of the jungle.'

'What have I to do?'

'You know very well. You hide and imitate the sound of truck motors.'

John protested, though only for appearance's sake, complaining he always had to play the part of a simple-minded enemy, but he finally resigned himself to sitting rather solemnly at the table, pretending to push several buttons, while little Thu, hiding under the bed, puffed out her cheeks to imitate the backfiring of engines. The game finished in an explosion of laughter and mad embraces.

This happened almost every day just before dinner, except when the B-52's on the neighbouring base took off at that same hour. On these evenings the inhuman roar dissipated the supernatural atmosphere in the bungalow, driving the shadows back to a world inaccessible to Thu's spirit and leaving her distraught in the solitude of her deserted lodgings, the forlorn grimace on her now aged face.

The meditations of the wise and the ingenuity applied by the whole population knew changing fortunes but were often crowned with success. In any case, in the high region 'operation rice fields' had been a complete triumph. The burnt areas were soon clothed in green, and the observers from the sky were unable to make out any difference between those covered by natural vegetation and the *rays* created by human hand. The Jarai had informed the Vietnamese of some of the thousands of ways conjured up by Ami for camouflaging paddy fields, and the inventive minds of the Vietnamese quickly devised others. For a long time the Americans had no suspicion of the precious collaboration they were providing their enemy.

The drivers and soldiers found a good part of their basic provisions on the spot, representing a not inconsiderable economy in transportation. As the bombings increased in intensity, it became possible to sow larger areas and thereby increase the complement of troops in the south.

It was all, as Ami often repeated, perched aloft in her solitary hut where Madame Ngha's emissaries kept her well informed of the smooth running of the operation, all thanks to the benevolence of the spirit of the earth, thanks to the patient reflections of man—and thanks to napalm.

4

THE HO CHI MINH WAY

I

Nonetheless, after the conventional bombing, which made a significant contribution in the form of venison, compensating in part for the grave damage still sometimes caused despite the skilful handling of the ears of the jungle, and after the scorching by napalm, which allowed the inexpensive and localized harvest of quantities of rice and manioc, the enemy began to use even more insidious and terrible weapons.

Eventually, either informed by its agents, or the aerial observers having perhaps detected some anomalies in the vegetation covering the burnt terrain, American intelligence came to realize, or at least surmise, that these clearings in the jungle had been used by their enemy in a very suspicious way. Thus alerted, the Pentagon demanded an increased effort from scientific research, which resulted in chemists perfecting weapons capable not only of destroying all living things, animal or plant, but of killing even the soil itself.

This method of waging war bore the title 'Biological Warfare'. The ingredients used had barbarous scientific names, but the general staff dubbed them with nicknames like blue agent, red agent, and purple agent, terms that Thu had managed to read in a secret memo and passed on to Madame Ngha. They were commonly known to the general public, however, under the simple and rather prudish name of defoliants. But their effects were not in fact limited to defoliation. They also devoured stalks and tree trunks and, penetrating gradually into the soil, attacked the roots themselves, destroying the very sources of life.

Wherever this pernicious and at times torrential shower descended, the trees quickly lost their foliage. Then beneath, the grass, bushes, and plants withered as if from leprosy, sinking into shapeless fragments on the ground. Finally even the strongest trunks were eaten by a horde of cancers, and their deepest roots so badly decayed that these giants of the jungle often met their end battered down by the monsoons or a staggering blow from a solitary elephant lost in this infernal place. To hasten the annihilation, this profanation of the forest and land was frequently followed, after a reasonable delay, by a bombardment of napalm and phosphorus, though this time lighter, since little remained to be consumed. The process rendered the place immaculate, leaving only ashes, but poisoned ashes, from which nothing could ever rise again, lying in a desolate landscape forbidden to all vegetation. This dead earth, it was clear, could no longer bear rice or manioc.

Yet for all this, traffic on the trail continued uninterrupted. The jungle was vast, and despite the power and abundance of his means, the enemy could destroy only a feeble part of it, a part which seemed immense if one of the devastated regions was crossed by foot or vehicle, but which must have appeared minute to observers gazing down upon the Annamite chain from high above. Enough cover always remained to conceal the convoys of arms and munitions.

Meanwhile, Madame Ngha, confronted with this new tactic, this perverse obstinacy on the part of the enemy in thwarting her best-laid plans, was in a constant state of indignation. She was furious at her inability to figure out how to 'transform bad into good', in accordance with the simple slogan she herself had launched in the Democratic Republic. This mortified and exasperated her. Van often had to bear the brunt of this ill-humour, though her boss almost always knew how to make amends; whenever a tear in the eye of her young secretary told her she had gone too far and caused her to reproach herself for this injustice, she would atone for it with a word or friendly gesture.

Later, when asked how she had found an answer to the

efoliant's agonizing challenge, how the very hideousness
f the scourge had inspired her with one of the most bril-
ant schemes of the war, Madame Ngha replied modestly
hat she had done it with the help of chance, chance aided
y the passionate interest she took in everything, even that
vhich seemed to have no direct connection with the con-
uct of the war.

She also declared that the idea had not come to her all at
nce; that a master plan had only emerged gradually, each
ntangible hint seeming insignificant at first; and that her
nly merit lay in not letting these hints vanish, but in
atiently collecting and coordinating them. It was Van, she
urther asserted, who had given the first impulse, and for
hat she would be eternally grateful.

Without her even being aware of it, chance had played a
ading role. One evening in her office near Hanoi she
ad been in a particularly foul mood at the steady flow of
iscouraging news and was so offensive to Van that she, no
onger able to stand the hostile atmosphere, burst into tears.
n the face of her distress, Madame Ngha's heart melted;
he bitterly reproached herself for this excess—unusual for her
-and, undergoing a severe self-criticism, acknowledged her
ults and apologized, finally embracing her secretary and
alling her her beloved sister.

'Now Van,' she said, 'you are going on a trip. It will
iean leaving me for a while, maybe three weeks or even a
ionth. I'll miss you, but I need to be alone to pull myself
gether and think things over. I must have someone reliable
ake an inspection in the south, especially in Cambodia, and
counted on sending Tuan, but you can go instead—you
now the situation just as well and it will do you good. It's
confidential mission but won't be very demanding. Take
dvantage of it to have a rest and enjoy yourself. I'll give
ou instructions and some letters of introduction tomorrow.
want you to have as pleasant a trip as possible, and I'll give
ppropriate orders.'

This was an example of how she could compensate for her

95

changes of mood with the most thoughtful attentions. Van dried her tears and thanked her effusively.

'On the way back make a detour into the high country, if you can, and see how our hill tribesmen are doing. It's been some time since I've had any news of Ami. Ask her what she thinks about these biological weapons. Maybe she'll have an idea—she often has excellent ones.'

Delighted at the prospect of this escapade, Van left a few days later, travelling with various convoys down the Ho Chi Minh Trail and being received at each way station with all the consideration due someone especially recommended by Madame Ngha. She arrived in the south without a hitch and, entering Cambodia, poked her thick spectacles every where anything interesting was to be seen; after a month's absence she returned by the same route, bringing back a thick notebook stuffed with entries from which, on the last days of her trip, she compiled a bulky report summarizing all the information of possible use to the service: condition of troops, morale, percentage of convoys reaching the south likelihood of an enemy attack in Cambodia, and so on.

Madame Ngha received her with open arms and, having read the report, congratulated her on the intelligence with which she had fulfilled her mission. She then began to ask her a host of questions about her trip.

'First—did you see Ami?'

'Yes, I saw her. She received me as if I were a great chief and sends you her highest regards. But as for the problem that's worrying us, the biological warfare, she couldn't make any suggestions.'

'I suspected that. It's not really within her province.'

'That's exactly what she said. I can tell you in her own words, since I memorized what the interpreter translated for me. "Ami is very sad at what is happening, for it seems the flying men are killing the earth. And when the earth is dead the spirit of the earth is no longer there. Ami can do nothing

96

without his aid." She added, "Tell the lady from Vietnam it is up to her to search, and I am sure she will find. Spirits other than those of the Jarai exist, like the spirit of the dead earth. But he lives in your world, not in mine. Ami is certain he will inspire your chief with favourable dreams." '

'That's what she said?' asked Madame Ngha, by no means smiling.

'Exactly.'

'Fine, so we'll put our faith in the *yang* of the dead earth. ... What else did you do? I did advise you to entertain yourself.'

'I did. Before leaving Cambodia I indulged in a long day tour.'

'You should have taken two or three days. Where did you go?'

'With a bit of conniving I managed to visit Angkor Wat, which I'd only seen before when I was little.'

'Tell me about it.'

Madame Ngha's curiosity, even for all kinds of useless information, was insatiable.

'There's not much to tell, I'm afraid, except that it's in a very sorry state.'

'Really? From the bombings?'

'Not at all. From the jungle.'

'The jungle?'

'Yes. The jungle's invading everywhere. Each day it causes more damage. It's really like a plague.'

'The jungle ... a plague,' repeated Madame Ngha.

Her tone had changed. This harmless sentence had gripped her attention in a surprising way. Why, she did not know. But it seemed to her that Van had uttered the words intentionally, as if her humble collaborator instinctively attributed to them some special significance, yet, unable to grasp this clearly herself, she had submitted them to her superior in the hope that she might.

Among the many qualities that had led Madame Ngha to choose Van as her secretary and confidante, this one she especially appreciated: that she often made the sort of comments which generated profitable ideas. She rarely made these ideas explicit herself, leaving this to the care of her chief. Was she utterly unconscious of the benefit Madame Ngha sometimes derived from her? Or was a superior intelligence hidden behind those glasses, restrained by modesty and an exceptional timidity? Madame Ngha often wondered, without ever quite being able to decide.

Whether Van was conscious of the potential promise in the little phrase 'really like a plague' or not, Madame Ngha asked her to relate her visit to the temple in detail, and listened carefully, her brow wrinkled with attention.

'The monk who acted as my guide never stopped bemoaning it. "We cannot do anything" he told me. "There are now only three of us living in these ruins to see to the upkeep. We would have to be three hundred to keep back the jungle— that or have equipment we just do not possess. The jungle is gradually eating away the stone. It is a plague worse than leprosy. Every vine we pull up grows back the next week. For every root dug out another shoots up with even more vigour." '

'Really?' said Madame Ngha in a faraway voice. 'This conscientious guardian finds the jungle a plague worse than leprosy?'

'You wouldn't be so surprised if you'd seen the terrible condition these wonders are in. If anything is left of them after the war, it will cost Cambodia a fortune to restore them.'

'A fortune,' agreed Madame Ngha in the same distant tone, 'a fortune to be free of the jungle ...'

A strange radiance illuminated her face and quickly faded. Impassive again, she changed the subject, as she often did when wishing to conceal her most intimate thoughts.

'The war is truly dreadful,' she said.

Van agreed unreservedly.

'Destruction on one side, waste on the other ... when funds are so precious.'

Van nodded and looked at her superior with curiosity.

'When peace returns, we too will have to spend a fortune on reconstruction—and not only on reconstruction—but to build a new country, Van. To create a united and magnificent Vietnam out of the ruins. That was Uncle Ho's first priority. He thought of the future at every moment, as we all must, of the future, of progress, of our development into a modern nation. Don't you agree, Van?'

'Yes, of course,' said the young secretary, staring at her, more and more intrigued.

'It's also the opinion of our President. He has called a meeting for next week to which I've been invited; our future will be the sole topic of discussion. He's asked each of the participants to think this over and submit proposals, since the war won't last forever and we must make preparations. I'm hoping heaven will inspire me this week with some interesting ideas, Van.'

She spoke with a vehemence she displayed only on certain occasions; when, for example, she foresaw the possibility of an elegant and subtle solution to some problem that bristled with difficulties. Van threw her a final odd glance, then modestly lowered her eyes and said: 'I'm sure Heaven will inspire you, Madame. Heaven or, as Ami put it, some of the spirits she believes in that don't haunt the Jarai world ... like the one she calls the Spirit of the Dead Earth.'

Madame Ngha did not object, and smiled.

2

Uncle Ho was dead. In his village the reconstructed house in which he had been born was piously maintained by a flock of nieces and nephews. In more elevated circles the new President continued to follow the policies of his predecessor and endeavoured to carry through some of his projects.

The unification of north and south, awaited for centuries and without which Uncle Ho had felt nothing great could become of Vietnam, stood out as the first of the day's problems. Though it would be necessary to wait for the end of the war to see it realized, in foreseeing that this end might occur sooner than anyone expected, the President was anxious to prepare the country for the new demands peace would impose and to accelerate plans for the future development of a regenerated Vietnam. Various measures had already been taken with this in mind.

The first had been the creation of a Ministry of Construction. At its head was placed one of the Republic's most competent engineers, one among those appreciated by the authorities not simply for their knowledge but also for their loftiness of vision and progressive spirit. Kim, a graduate of a great Western university who had worked for a number of years in the United States on gigantic public-works projects, was better qualified than anyone else for this post. Armed with the best technical knowledge, with experience, and beyond that, with enthusiasm at the prospect of creation, Kim had settled down to his task in a country where practically everything still remained to be done. Unfortunately, this task was surrounded by difficulties.

He revealed some of them to Madame Ngha, who went to visit him a few days before the conference arranged by the President to discuss precisely these problems. She had a very high opinion of Minister Kim, and having in the past few days developed some personal and original views on the subject of public works, she wanted to compare them with his.

'One can always dream up projects,' said Kim, appearing discouraged. 'I've done some fine ones I think, or grand ones, anyway. It's not imagination I lack, and I have specialists at my service as competent as any in the West. I'll submit these plans at the meeting—but I'm afraid they won't be accepted.'

'Why not?'

'Money. To accomplish what I would like for this country —road systems, electrification, new cities—we'd need enormous sums that just won't be there after the war.'

'I notice,' she interrupted, 'that you put road systems first.'

'They're essential. It's the first step to take if we're ever to become a modern nation....'

He explained why. She was delighted to find that the ideas of this minister and technologist corresponded so closely with her own on this point. Save that to her the financial problem did not appear insoluble.

'In other countries they have carried out grandiose projects even starting from scratch.'

'Starting from scratch, Ngha, that's it!' shouted Kim. 'I see what you mean. Desert countries. But don't you understand? That's the dream of every builder! If only the gods had made Vietnam a desert. Here our greatest enemy is— the jungle!'

She trembled. This outburst accorded so well with her own thinking that she was not far from seeing in it a miraculous coincidence. As Kim went on, an idea began to take concrete shape in her mind.

'Seventy per cent of our land is covered with jungle, Ngha, and that's a terrible handicap for a modern country. To build cities, factories, roads, all the things necessary for even regional development, it will cost us more to clear the jungle than it would for the actual construction itself, and on top of that we must anticipate considerable yearly expenses just to keep it back.'

'Would you explain your problems to me calmly, Kim?' she said. 'I don't understand much about public works, but I sometimes have intuitions, and it's not impossible that I might give you a hand. Besides, you know the President often listens to my opinions and takes them seriously.'

Kim could hardly have asked for more. He knew Madame Ngha's support was the best possible guarantee of success.

'As you observed, the most urgent problem is the road

system. That's where we'll have to put our initial effort once peace has returned. Now then ...'

'I completely agree,' broke in Madame Ngha.

'I too think the problem of avenues of communication ought to be tackled first,' she said after taking a sip of tea. 'Comrade Kim has just given us the technical reasons. They seem irrefutable to me, and I would venture to add these....'

The conference gathered around the President some of the highest-ranking figures of the Republic and Party, including two representatives of the provisional government in the south. The military was excluded (the subject was *con*struction) except, of course, for Madame Ngha, whose activities extended into every sphere, military and civilian. The President welcomed them all cordially, with a friendly word for everybody. Then he had tea served. After a few polite exchanges he set forth briefly the purpose of the meeting: to define a programme of construction and development for the country. Minister Kim was allowed to speak first.

He described his project in broad outline, emphasizing that he had drawn it up with a view to the development of the country as a whole, and not just that of a few privileged areas. He concluded his presentation by laying stress on the urgency for an adequate road system, the backbone of which was to be a major axial highway crossing the Annamite chain from north to south. He was deeply convinced of its necessity, and after several conversations together, he and Madame Ngha had decided to argue this course, backing each other up if necessary.

The President nodded pensively, then asked the opinion of each of those present. Everyone approved of the spirit in which Kim had worked. Only the Minister of Finance seemed to have any reservations, but he stated he would present them later when he had a better idea of certain other aspects of the plan.

When her turn came, Madame Ngha spoke rather longer than anyone else.

'To the excellent technical reasons Comrade Kim has just given us,' she said, 'it seems to me others could be added, of a completely different nature, but perhaps equally important. To begin with, the major north-south axis that has just been described will be seen as a symbol of unification.'

'But don't we have the old route, the one that used to be called the Mandarin Way?' objected the Minister of Finance. 'No doubt it could be repaired and enlarged at much less expense than your mountain highway.'

'Certainly,' replied Kim, 'but it would clearly be inadequate for our development.'

'And to content ourselves with a road constructed by and for the colonialists,' continued Madame Ngha, 'would be a narrow-minded policy, and bad from a psychological point of view. It would only serve the already privileged regions of the plain. Don't we want to create a new Vietnam?'

Sensing approval in a gesture from the President, she went on: 'Furthermore, and above all else, we don't want the population of the mountains left in isolation. They have been scorned for too long, and besides, we now have them on our side. It is our duty and would also be in our interest to help them benefit from the leap forward that will follow victory. We must create new facilities and occupations for them. We could construct vacation resorts for the plains people there, or I should say here, as there will only be one Vietnam, and centres of attraction for foreigners, whose curiosity will lead them to this world-famous mountain range. For you can be sure we are going to see a flood of tourists when the war is over. There will be no need for advertising; the legend of the Ho Chi Minh Trail will be enough. The big game, so plentiful in these mountains, will also attract hunters. And in the long run this will all pay for itself, on condition that we can provide suitable roads and railways. In conclusion, it seems to me this north-south axis, which would connect Hanoi and Saigon by way of the mountains, has to be our first achievement.'

Her eloquence and sense of conviction were winning the assembly over. All seemed possessed by this evocation of the future. She glanced at Kim, who perceived it was now his turn to carry the argument further.

'Comrade Ngha,' he said, 'has explained much better than I possibly could the many reasons that lead me to recommend this plan. But you can see the whole thing better from this map.'

He picked up a long roll of paper he had placed in a corner of the room on his arrival, and asked the President's permission to put it up at the back of the room. Climbing up on a chair, he fixed it to the wall. Everyone's eyes settled on a large-scale map of Indochina, with long contours traced in multicoloured lines.

'Here are the future roads, the roads of a new Vietnam,' said Kim as he jumped down.

This map had been drawn up to represent the essential aspects of this part of his project, so that the major road system stood out in clear relief. It had been done at the request of Madame Ngha, who had taken a close interest in this diagram, at times suggesting some modification of detail. Kim and his engineers had always listened respectfully to her suggestions and followed them whenever possible.

The result was impressive, well designed to stagger the mind and capture the imagination. Everyone was enraptured and aroused. Without giving them time to recover, Kim seized a bamboo ruler and indicated the main points as he commented on the map's principal features.

'This is the major north-south highway, to be the main artery of Vietnam. From it will originate all the secondary routes, which you can see here, linking us with Thailand via Laos, with Burma, with our friends the Chinese, and, on the other side towards the east, with our reconstructed ports.'

A scarlet line a quarter of an inch wide represented this gigantic highway, which began at Hanoi, met the Annamite chain a little farther down, traversed the whole of the high region, edged along the Laotian and Cambodian frontiers, and finally regained the plain at Saigon, having crossed the whole of the Indochinese peninsula from north to south.

'The blue line parallel to the first one,' continued Kim, 'is the railway, serving the high region as well. As for the green line ...'

This was the course of a high-tension line that would take power to the hinterlands.

'You can see that the blue and green lines follow the highway for most of the total distance. We wanted this wherever the terrain permitted, since our study shows it's the most economical solution. Even if the railway and power lines are not constructed until later, it would cost less to excavate a single strip of jungle wide enough for all three lanes than to make three separate, narrower ones. I can assure you that neither I nor my collaborators have ever lost sight of this problem of economy....'

At this moment the Minister of Finance made a sign as if to speak. Madame Ngha immediately forestalled him.

'An idea has just occurred to me,' she said, '... but first I must apologize. It's not something for me to decide—it will be up to our Comrade President, the whole meeting, and the people.'

'Tell us your idea,' insisted the President.

'Well, I thought we might already give a name to this fine creation of Comrade Kim. What would you say to the Ho Chi Minh Route, in memory of the famous trail?'

This proposition was greeted with general enthusiasm, but some of the advisers then began to ponder.

'Route?' said one. 'It's certainly much more than a route. Perhaps we could call it the Ho Chi Minh Highway or Auto Route?'

This had been irrelevant to Madame Ngha from the moment the venerated name became associated in their minds with the realization of the project. She was now sure it would not be rejected. There was a silence, broken suddenly by the President himself.

'The Ho Chi Minh Way,' he cried out, 'that's it. First of all, it's not only a road. And also, "The Way" symbolizes the whole existence of our dear departed. "The Ho Chi Minh Way", that's how I propose to consecrate this magnificent project.'

'The Ho Chi Minh Way,' they all repeated piously.

The name was adopted. Madame Ngha and Kim again exchanged a glance of complicity, certain of their victory in spite of the objections the Finance Minister was asking permission to present.

'Has an estimate been made?' he demanded.

Kim looked somewhat embarrassed, and then began by making several excuses.

'An approximate estimate, subject to many modifications. The figure is very high. Much higher than it would be in a Western country, where nature has already been conquered and kept under control for a long time. There, new roads only have to cross fields, pastures, or patches of forest that are nothing compared to ours. Here, virgin forest covers the mountains and thrusts primordial roots into the soil, every last one of which must be eradicated before any construction can begin. That, more than anything else, will be very expensive.'

'How expensive?' asked the President.

After hesitating, Kim mentioned an enormous figure, provisional, of course, but unfortunately to be considered a minimum. The President sighed. In the profound silence that followed, the Finance Minister, himself deeply grieved, stated that his conscience forced him to consider the project unrealizable, at least until many years after the war. The resources at Vietnam's disposal, even including considerable aid from friendly countries, would only make it possible to contemplate a small fraction of this enterprise. His words had the effect of a cold shower, and gloomy despondency displaced their enthusiasm.

Kim threw an imploring glance at Madame Ngha. The

worried President himself turned to ask her opinion, as he so often did on delicate matters. She took another sip of tea and announced: 'I think Comrade Kim's project is perfect. However, we cannot doubt the wisdom of our comrade, the Finance Minister, if he finds it too heavy a burden for us.'

'So?' asked the President, disappointed.

'So, perhaps in thinking over this aspect of the problem, and given the present circumstances, we might come up with a method for realizing the same plan, but under more economic conditions.'

'Does Kim believe that's possible?'

'Not with the means at our disposal.'

'So?'

'Here I must again let Madame Ngha speak,' said the minister, smiling and bowing towards her. 'Judging from the hints she has given me, she has material means I don't possess and spiritual resources far surpassing those of engineers.'

3

At the centre in Thailand the day generally passed without an alert. It was rare that an ear of the jungle transmitted any signal. The convoys moved only at night; the animals and insects of the tropical forest slept, stupefied by the heat. Confronted with this dreary silence, the monitoring staff also found it difficult to keep from falling asleep.

General Bishop took advantage of this calm to write up a report on the latest results. Thu sat at her desk typing a memo. Both were startled when Colonel Shaw rushed in at such an unexpected hour.

'Trucks?'

'Better than that, sir. A conversation—in Vietnamese, and incredibly clear.'

'I knew we'd have a chance like this one day. Put it through, fast. Thu, you listen.'

The conversation immediately came in over the loud-speaker and was simultaneously recorded on tape for future reference. Thu, meanwhile, began translating, her brow creased with attention. The IBM S 360/65 was cut into the circuit. A red point on the screen indicated the transmitter's position: north of the seventeenth parallel, near the Laotian frontier, a region the American intelligence service already suspected, and one where a dense network of ears of the jungle had been dropped in the past few weeks.

'My back's killing me, Comrade,' translated Thu. 'I've been stacking crates all night with my team. Crate after crate of munitions.'

'I know, Comrade. Last month we were on fatigue for four nights running ourselves. The large tunnel was already half full then. . . .'

'A tunnel,' interrupted the general, 'I suspected there was one in this area. . . .'

Thu cut him short with a gesture of apology, trying not to lose the thread.

'It's more than three-quarters full now, and most of the caves are packed to bursting. . . .'

'Caves, I was sure of it,' inserted the general again.

'There's only a little space left in number twelve, but . . .'

Here the voice abruptly faded. Thu stopped. General Bishop took the opportunity to summarize the situation.

'It's a conversation between two soldiers, and establishes an important point. We suspected there were supplies deeply buried in this region. Now we're sure and know their exact location . . . to be precise, hill 873,' he added, leaning over the screen.

He fell silent, for the dialogue had resumed, but in a different tone. The two men were now practically whisper-ing, and with a skilful adjustment Shaw attempted to make

heir voices distinct. He succeeded and Thu went on: 'That's
General Hoan himself coming this way. He arrived this
morning to make an inspection of the centre.'

'Hoan!' shouted General Bishop, 'He's the one in charge
of transport....'

'And do you know the two others with him?'

'There's a man and a woman. No, I don't know them
.. at least not the woman, but the man is also a general, a
high ranking general.... It's—no, it can't be true, comrade!'

'Yes, I tell you, it's him. I'm sure....'

'Giap! Impossible!'

The soldier had lowered his voice again, so low that Thu
had to cup her hand behind her ear to hear him.

'Giap! Impossible!'

This time it was General Bishop who yelled triumphantly.
With a look Thu begged him to keep quiet. The first soldier
went on in the same confidential tone.

'I tell you, it's him. I know the woman too. It's Madame
Ngha.'

'Madame Ngha!' the second soldier and General Bishop
cried at the same time, the one in a whisper several hundred
miles away, the other at the top of his voice in his office.

'It's her, I'm sure. I've seen her before. She was Uncle
Ho's right arm. She's still the President's most influential
adviser.'

'Madame Ngha!' repeated the general, breathless with surprise and excitement.

The name of Madame Ngha was not unfamiliar to him.
The intelligence service did not know all that much about
her, except that she was among the most important of Vietnam's mysterious leaders.

'They're coming in this direction,' murmured one of the
soldiers.

'It's better if they don't find us here. We're off duty, all
right, but they might think we're trying to eavesdrop.'

The voices died away. Only the crunching of brush under-
foot could be heard.

'My God,' shouted the general, praying passionately, 'gi⟨...⟩
us a miracle. Make them stop near the sensor. Oh God, l⟨...⟩
us hear what they're going to say!'

Near hill 873 two secret-service agents, dressed in soldier⟨...⟩
uniforms to give them a better feel for their roles, gre⟨...⟩
silent at a peremptory signal from Dr. Wang. The sce⟨...⟩
being played was of such importance that the physicist ha⟨...⟩
wanted to direct it himself, unwilling to leave the respon⟨...⟩
bility to any of his assistants. Isolated in a glass booth set ⟨...⟩
that same morning in this deserted corner of the jungle, t⟨...⟩
Chinese scientist controlled the response and simultaneo⟨...⟩
transmission of a live ear of the jungle, previously modifi⟨...⟩
for this with caution and skill. Following a scenario work⟨...⟩
out in advance and already rehearsed several times, at anoth⟨...⟩
signal from him the agents rose and moved slowly away.

A trio consisting of General Hoan, Madame Ngha, a⟨...⟩
Giap (it actually was he) listened in silence some distan⟨...⟩
away. In his booth Dr. Wang pressed several buttons, a⟨...⟩
his voice, strangely distorted by the loud-speakers, reverb⟨...⟩
ated through the jungle.

'We can talk now,' he said, 'I've cut the ear out of t⟨...⟩
circuit. We have to give you time to move closer. I think i⟨...⟩
worked.

'It was perfect,' agreed Madame Ngha.

'It's your turn now. Will you take your places?'

The three went over towards the place near the ear of t⟨...⟩
jungle just occupied by the soldiers.

'Do you want to test out your voices?' Dr. Wang ask⟨...⟩
amiably.

'God's on our side,' babbled General Bishop.

He was seized, almost overwhelmed, by such frenzi⟨...⟩
gratitude at heaven's bestowing so miraculous a blessing tha⟨...⟩
hands tortuously clasped, his whole body trembled. Sha⟨...⟩

was in better control of himself, though just as amazed at this technological miracle that made it possible to listen in to a confidential discussion among the highest enemy leaders. Thu remained calm but showed deep interest as she translated the great commander-in-chief's words, spoken with cool authority.

'General Hoan,' said Giap, 'we must have three more caverns deepened and made ready. I want them the same capacity as the other twelve. We are expecting a lot more supplies in the next few weeks.'

'I'll see to that,' replied Hoan. 'We have enough cement, but may I be permitted to make a remark? There are considerable stocks here already. Isn't it unwise to store too large a proportion of our equipment and reserve munitions in the same place? As the Western saying goes "Don't put all your eggs in one basket."'

Madame Ngha's melodious voice then echoed through this sanctuary of American intelligence. General Bishop was unable to suppress a shiver of delight. Thu, smiling imperceptibly, trembled ever so slightly before translating her words.

'In response to that proverb, General Hoan, a very wise man of the New World (they still existed a hundred years ago) retorted: "Put all your eggs in one basket, and keep an eye on the basket."'

'Mark Twain!' blurted out Colonel Shaw heedlessly, pleased at the chance to show that from time to time he read a work of literature.

The general silenced him with a furious glare.

'Our reserves are safest here,' said Giap. 'The caves are under thirty feet of rock and ten feet of concrete. That's enough to protect them from the most violent bombing. None of the other depots are as secure.'

'Even those at Datum and Chau?' asked Madame Ngha's gentle voice. 'We still have a fair amount of matériel here....'

'Yes, and I shudder to think that the enemy might someday discover them, because, between us' (here Giap lowered his voice) 'they are extremely vulnerable. . . .'

'Datum and Chau! Get that down, get that down!' yelled General Bishop, so totally out of his mind with joy that he completely forgot this priceless information was being taped and there was no chance of its being lost.

General Hoan kept his eyes riveted on Madame Ngha. She signalled it was his turn to reply. He was visibly ill at ease, and a drop of sweat appeared now and then on his forehead. He was not accustomed to speaking directly in front of a microphone, still less before an ear of the jungle, and like an amateur was at times completely paralysed with stage fright. The piercing, insistent stares of his two companions (Madame Ngha's suddenly expressed cold ferocity) were necessary to keep him from missing his turn.

'I wasn't thinking of the bombings,' he said, 'I know very well the tunnels and caves are invulnerable from that point of view, but what I'm afraid of is . . .'

'What are you afraid of, then?'

He stumbled occasionally, despite the fact that a piece of paper with all his responses on it had been fixed to a board in front of him. Madame Ngha had reluctantly agreed to let him use a text, worried that a complete lapse of memory on his part, or some even more dangerous blunder, might risk alerting the enemy. Giap himself carried it off perfectly naturally; she did even better, sustaining the conversation any time Hoan weakened, like an experienced actress who knew all the tricks of her trade that might rescue a hesitant beginner. She had decided to include the head of transport in her scenario, despite his evident lack of talent for this kind of exercise, and Giap had agreed. A dialogue simply between her and the commander-in-chief would not have permitted certain remarks, certain details, to come up naturally; they would, on the other hand, have actually been required in the presence of a subordinate who was not exactly well informed about the situation. Anyway, she had assumed, and rightly so, that Hoan's hesitations could easily be accounted for by his excitement at speaking with two of the most important people in Vietnam.

'I am afraid,' he continued with a little more assurance, 'that the enemy might finally become informed of the immensity of these supplies, as well as the futility of bombing them, and then decide to launch a ground attack.'

'Believe me . . .' said Madame Ngha.

Thu translated every nuance of the conversation perfectly and seemed to delight in rendering Giap's authority, the agitation of Hoan, and now Madame Ngha's rather disdainful irony.

'Believe me, the commander-in-chief has foreseen every possibility and in particular that one.'

Here Giap gave a low, sarcastic laugh, full of scorn for the transport chief's naïveté, which Thu, caught up in the rhythm of the dialogue, faithfully reproduced.

'Don't worry,' he said condescendingly, 'my staff and I have already considered the possibility of an attack by ground forces, and Madame Ngha, who, as you know, is always well informed, does not think it at all impossible. If it happens, and we almost wish it would, let me tell you that our élite troops are ready to cross the Mu-Mok Pass to confront the invader, defend our supplies and inflict a terrible loss on the enemy.

'The Mu-Mok Pass, get that down, write that down!' shouted General Bishop again.

'I understand,' said General Hoan. 'I'll have work begun on the new caverns today.'

Over in his glass booth Dr. Wang raised his arm. The three dignitaries stopped speaking and moved away from the ear of the jungle, making the same soft rustle in the grass as the soldiers.

4

'Shaw!' bellowed the general, 'get General Headquarters on my direct line immediately. They must be informed at once ... this is priceless information, and if they know how to use it up there, it could change the whole course of the war. I'm sure I don't need to advise absolute secrecy.... Thu, have the tapes given to you. I want a complete translation of the whole conversation—not a word left out. Can you get it done by this evening?'

'Certainly, sir.'

'As for you, Shaw, my congratulations. Top marks for you and your assistants. This is a master stroke.'

'We were lucky, sir,' the colonel said modestly. 'We have to admit that.'

'I admit it, extraordinarily lucky. But you still have to have an absolutely faultless technique to be able to take advantage of it. And that's what has happened. Let the whole staff know I'm extremely satisfied, and that I'm proud of them.'

Shaw nodded and went to convey the general's congratulations, especially to the technician who had caught the precious conversation. This stimulated feverish competition and redoubled efforts, which soon brought results. A few hours later, as night fell, the colonel was again able to announce that several trucks had been detected. The general listened to the noise for a moment, then looked at the screen and concluded that a long convoy was heading straight towards the notorious hill 873. He did not carry the operation any further however, since he had spoken with the authorities in the meantime and received precise instructions for coping with just such a contingency.

'They're going to fill up the tunnels and caves, Shaw, that's obvious, and we have to let them go ahead and do it. We're not to bomb this area for a while. Orders from General Headquarters. I can't say any more about it—top secret—except that a heavy blow, a decisive blow, is being prepared. But don't let that encourage you to relax the monitoring. It's never been more valuable.'

Thu handed him the translation she had just finished. The general grabbed it and dismissed her, ordering the young girl not to return to the office that night. He would not need her any longer; she had worked all day and deserved a free evening. As for him, he did not take a moment's rest but, after having a sandwich brought to him, began drafting a report for General Headquarters. In it he transcribed the conversations and accompanied them with a long commentary of his own.

Thu, her face unusually animated as she muttered to herself, went back to her bungalow in the dark, walking briskly, almost running at times in her haste to share a message with her beloved beings.

'Thi Hai!'

She had arrived a little out of breath and spoke in an undertone, torn between regret at waking the children if they were already asleep and the desire to announce the good news that very night.

'Madame?'

'Are John and Thu asleep?'

She had decided some time ago that little Thu would sleep every night in John's room, since it was far more comfortable than her parents' hut. The little girl was fragile and did not adapt well to sleeping on a mat under a straw roof.

The ghostly Thi Hai reassured her: 'I've put them to bed, but they're not asleep yet, Madame. I heard them laughing and whispering just a moment ago.'

'Good! I have to tell them something.... Come along, Thi Hai, you should know too....'

She hurried into the room, half lifted the mosquito net, and, leaning over the bed, implanted two fervent kisses as she passionately clasped the emptiness.

'Thu, guess who I spoke to this afternoon.... You'll never guess. You won't either, John ... Aunt Ngha!'

'Madame Ngha!' Thi Hai exclaimed behind her.

'Aunt Ngha!' shouted little Thu opening her eyes wide, which till then she had kept tightly closed, pretending to be asleep.

'Herself. I heard her. I talked to her just as I'm talking to you.'

'What did she say?'

'She said to give you a kiss, both you and John. She said she thinks of you often, of all of us; you too, Thi Hai. She added that you must forgive her if she doesn't speak to you herself, but she's very busy at the moment.'

'What's she doing?' asked John, opening his eyes too.

'She's thinking up new games.'

'When can we play them?'

'They're games for grownups this time. But she's promised to try and find one we can all play together.... And now you must hurry up and go to sleep.'

The two children smiled at her and closed their eyes. She planted two more kisses on the pillow, then carefully lowered the mosquito net and crept out on tiptoe

General Bishop had almost finished his report when again Colonel Shaw burst into his office.

'Listen, sir.'

'Another convoy? Conversations?'

'Better than that, sir,' said the exultant colonel.

Stimulated by the day's successes and his superior's congratulations, he had spent much of the night having new attempts made to penetrate, with circuits of still greater complexity, even deeper and more subtle enemy secrets. When the loud-speaker was connected a soft but distinct humming was heard in the office. The general reacted instinctively: shaking his head, he waved his hand as if to brush away an obtrusive insect.

'A window must have been left open,' he grumbled, 'I gave specific orders ...'

The colonel's triumphant laugh cut him short.

'A mosquito, sir! But not here—out there. Never before has our technique been so perfect. It's a day of firsts. I didn't think you'd want to miss this.'

Hesitant, the general looked at him in silence, wondering whether, at the very moment he was preparing a report that would probably lead to important decisions for the conduct of the war, it was proper to give time to anything so trivial. Finally, he concluded it was, and listened reverently in a kind of trance. The miracle of science that permitted him to hear in his own office the buzz of a minute insect deep in the heart of the jungle seemed to him to deserve the homage of a few moments' silent attention. After a minute or so, having congratulated and thanked Shaw, he furtively made an entry in the notebook he kept for material relating to his book *On Monitoring the Indochinese Jungle*, where this phenomenon went to join, with the usual effusive comments, the snarl of a tiger on the prowl and the triumphal ballet of an elephant in the moonlight.

5

Following the information communicated to it by Service S, information that confirmed its own suspicions regarding the enemy munitions buried deep in the mountains and protected from even the most violent bombing, the American High

Command decided to launch a full-scale ground attack against what appeared to be the principal depot—hill 873.

The troops would consist of South Vietnamese units. American air support would be massive; all the techniques refined to perfection since the advent of Biological Warfare would be used on the dense jungle that covered the mountains from the Mu-Mok Pass up to the notorious depot. This was the route the enemy shock troops were to follow; the intelligence provided by General Bishop left no doubt on that score. It was here the High Command had decided to strike, thus killing two birds with one stone: destroying the supplies and annihilating the élite troops lured into the ambush. It would further result in the complete destruction of a trail undoubtedly very useful to the North Vietnamese, putting it out of service for a long period.

Madame Ngha, with the idea of inspiring just such a tactic on the part of her adversary, had manoeuvred too well to be caught unawares when various signs confirmed that this had in fact become their plan.

One indication, and not the least significant, was supplied by a high-ranking functionary of the Chinese intelligence service with whom she maintained cordial relations. He had asked to see her in order to convey, so his message said, some information that had recently fallen into his hands and that he had genuine reason to believe important.

She took care not to miss their appointment; it was held in China not far from the border. The Vietnamese woman was received in the private room of a restaurant where the Chinese official was certain their conversation would not be overheard. Neither the war nor their positions exempted them from greeting one another with the usual compliments and tokens of courtesy. Ky asked his guest to sit down at a table already laden with dishes full of delicacies, all cold. He apologized for this affront, but their time was valuable, and what he had to reveal must not be overheard by any of the waiters.

They both sat down at the table. After a few more commonplace remarks, Ky came round to the real object of their discussion.

'It has come to my attention that your enemy, and ours, is preparing a ground attack against the substantial supplies you have accumulated near hill 873. Perhaps that doesn't come as a great surprise to you.'

She admitted good-naturedly she was not all that astonished, even professing she had feared such a possibility for some time.

'But,' she added, 'I don't have any precise details on what preparations the enemy might be making.'

Ky stared at her thoughtfully, as if trying to weigh the exact proportion of truth and evasiveness in this last assertion. Then he went on: 'It just so happens I have a few details myself. My service has managed to capture an American message in a code we've had the key to for some time. In brief, the message said that the attack on your depot at hill 873 would be launched by the South Vietnamese using powerful American air support, including helicopters. The date is almost set: two months before the rainy season. In principle it will be limited to the period before that season begins. This is stated quite clearly in the message. The main objective will be the destruction of your supplies.'

'Thank you for such valuable information,' said Madame Ngha. 'I'll pass it on to High Command, who will no doubt make good use of it.'

'But that's not all.'

'Really?' said Madame Ngha, maintaining her impassivity.

'This is certainly even more important: we're convinced the Americans knew we'd intercept this message and were capable of decoding it.'

'Then it's just a trick: make us believe they are aiming at one point while an attack is being prepared for another?'

Her forehead creased worriedly as if out of profound disillusionment.

'No, that's not it. The attack is definitely going to be on hill 873. We're sure of that.'

Madame Ngha's face relaxed.

'Then what would be the reason for this deliberate indiscretion?'

'I see at least two reasons: first, the Americans want to be sure that we won't intervene directly as long as their offensive has only a limited objective. This I know for certain: the point was discussed semi-officially by diplomats in Vientiane after this "secret" became common knowledge. . . .'

'And the Americans were right,' she said in so neutral a tone that her phrase could just as easily pass for a question as a simple statement of the obvious. 'You have no intention of intervening under those conditions.'

'They are right as far as that goes. The war is one thing, and politics another. Our advisers have managed to convince the authorities responsible that in this case it would be inept to intervene, as much for our sake as yours.'

'I just wanted to be sure. . . . But you mentioned two reasons?'

'There is one other possibility, but we don't have any way to confirm it. It's simply a personal opinion, or rather an impression. It's obvious the Americans also knew that nothing would be more urgent for us than to communicate information of this importance to you. So? . . . So,' he continued with a smile, 'I won't offend you by supposing for even a second that you haven't already reached the same conclusion as me.'

'No offence,' she said, 'it's clear that, forewarned in this way, we would take measures to defend our depot at hill 873.'

'I knew Madame Ngha would never be fooled by such a trick and would take the measures necessary to avoid such a trap.'

'I will think about it,' she said, returning his smile.

6

'When are they going to get moving?' grumbled General Bishop. 'We're all ready. The defoliants are bound to have had their effect by now. What are they waiting for?'

For the third week since the South Vietnamese had attacked, Service S was on edge. The general almost never left his office and lived in a state of constant excitement, for the ears of the jungle were busy too. The signals from one after another were almost continuous and allowed them to follow, by means of cross-checking and skilful interpolation, the movement of enemy troops advancing minute by minute, hour by hour, foot by foot towards hill 873.

On the very first day of the offensive a light advance guard consisting of infantry and a few reconnaissance vehicles had crossed the Mu-Mok Pass and marched rapidly in the direction of the depot. This would prove useful, since they marked out the trail to be followed later by the main body of troops. As a result, General Bishop had been in a position to begin the process of complete defoliation over most of his area more than two weeks before. Night after night a dense shower of pernicious substances fell silently over this trail with the customary precision made possible by the ears of the jungle.

The insidious action of the chemicals persisted until the fibrous husks full of half-dead sap were ready to catch fire and devour everything at the first blast of napalm. This was in fact the next stage of the American plan: a bombardment with incendiaries as soon as the main body of enemy troops, with its columns of transports, heavy equipment, and artillery, had advanced far enough along the trail.

This mass of troops now appeared to be marking time on the near side of the pass. The ears of the jungle continued to signal only the presence of light units in the area prepared for complete annihilation. The South Vietnamese themselves progressed towards hill 873, encountering little resistance even being restrained by their own command as they waited for the right moment to deal their double-edged mortal blow. General Bishop was baffled and strained at the bit.

'Could they suspect anything?' he murmured impatiently. 'This snail's pace isn't like them.'

As a matter of fact, there were several reasons for the delay. The scenario was exceedingly complex this time, demanding varied and delicate nuances in the different recordings as well as a special dexterity on the part of its director to make it appear natural. Moreover, it unfolded on two separate fronts, with the élite troops (the real ones, those Giap intended to pit against the aggressors) having to make a rather long detour through Laos to escape enemy surveillance. Dr. Wang had had to put on quite an ingenious virtuoso performance, for it was no longer a simple matter of the commonplace rumble of a few truck engines. A whole range of sound effects was required to create the proper illusion: a small advance guard on some tracks; a well-equipped army with heavy weapons and motorized units on others. Perfection here could only be attained after a long and intensive effort of imagination, for such creative work demanded time, even for one so exceptionally gifted at it. The final aim could only be achieved through a subtle symphony in which a complete register of metallic noises harmonized with a chorus of skilfully rehearsed conversations between soldiers, noncommissioned and commissioned officers and orders, significant but not suspicious, issued by NCOs (Thu was not idle during this period either. General Bishop kept her around as much as possible, so much did he fear missing some scrap of conversation that might call for a immediate response; but this additional work, with its long hours of nightly attendance, did not seem to tire her. On the contrary, it was obvious she took a greater and more sustained interest in her work.)

These tapes then had to be carefully and rationally distributed along the route staked out by hundreds of ears of the jungle, so that the advance would appear to progress normally; the whole was made to sound coherent by previously adjusting the tape recorders with a suitable time-lapse. As a preliminary to this, of course, all the ears had had to be located, a formidable task. But several teams of specialists, aided by detecting devices invented by the Chinese scientist, had now been trained for this. They worked more rapidly than the hill tribesmen, and just as effectively.

Yet this was not all there was to the first stage of the operation. Despite the length of this section of jungle, Madame Ngha still wanted it strewn with wreckage that would appear on the aerial photos after the raid. The plan for total destruction, which she now knew in detail, first from having suggested it and then from Thu's reports, did not leave the Americans much chance of spotting many remains after the strike, but they would still be astonished not to see some traces of metal tank treads, cannon barrels, or at the very least a few truck frames emerging from the bed of ashes. These objects therefore were transported silently to the spot. As always, Madame Ngha looked far ahead, anticipating future operations. Some of her collaborators were inclined to believe the enemy gullible enough to attribute the absence of wreckage to the excellence of his own methods of annihilation. But she was careful to avoid the trap of underestimating her adversary, and preferred to keep all the trumps on her side, even if it did mean an additional effort.

'Those damned storms again!' muttered the general.

One of the monitoring personnel had just reported a violent tornado in which an almost uninterrupted succession of thunderclaps punctuated the roar of a continuous torrent beating down on the forest. It was in Laos, far from the theatre of operations, but where a few ears of the jungle had been haphazardly scattered anyway. Out of curiosity the general had the noise piped in, and listened for a few moments.

'But the rainy season's not here yet,' he commented. It's not due for more than a month.'

Thu hastily intervened: 'That sort of thing's quite common in upper Laos, sir.'

She explained that the rains usually came on a fairly precise date but that it wasn't at all rare for a few isolated storms to occur in certain parts of Indochina, especially, she insisted, in this particular area of Laos. Reassured and always glad to learn something new, the general simply remarked: 'That makes two nights in a row. I hope the weather won't be bad in the area around hill 873. The planes wouldn't be able to play their part.... Now there's a hurricane as well.'

'One frequently goes with the other, sir. But it won't last long.'

The thunder, the downpour, the hurricane were all sounds Dr. Wang's assistants had carefully recorded during the previous monsoon and kept in reserve for just such an important occasion as this, the camouflaging of a powerful army's, the real army's, approach as it marched towards hill 873 by a roundabout route. Besides this unleashing of the elements, the Chinese scientist's department possessed a range of sound effects extensive enough to allow infinite variation, thus eliminating the risk of attracting attention by suspicious repetition. The sound of rain alone, for example, itself composed a symphony of ever-renewed harmonies, from the dull sonorousness of heavy drops falling on the rigid leaves of wild banana trees to the sharp patter of a sudden shower on the fine grass of a forest clearing.

'It's pretty unlikely in the region we're worried about, sir,' insisted Thu. 'One or two, maybe even three thunderstorms this season—it's happened before. But many more would be quite exceptional.'

It was in this way she conveyed Madame Ngha's prudence, for she had given instructions to discontinue the storms the following nights. To replace them Dr. Wang had kept in reserve other concerts such as croaking frogs or the cries of flying foxes at twilight, when the shadows allowed men to move in the jungle without danger of being spotted by enemy aircraft, as well as a great variety of crickets, of course; there was also the deafening hoot of a troop of gibbons, generally heard only at sunrise but sometimes (as Thu would affirm to General Bishop, avid for such details) provoked at night by an especially starlit sky or perhaps by the uneasy dream of one of them, which would then arouse the entire tribe and unleash a cacophony that might last for hours.

Enthralled by his secretary's explanations, the general was patiently awaiting the night's events when Colonel Shaw entered the office with the expression he saved for moments of triumph.

'Sir! It's happened. The main army's on the march. They're moving through the pass and advancing rapidly. Troops, tanks, motorized artillery, everything!'

'At last!' roared the general. 'We've got them. Send the sound through.'

7

Madame Ngha, in the process of examining a set of photos that had just arrived, asked Van to read her Thu's latest report. Though continuing her scrutiny, she did not miss a single word.

—'Headquarters has sent us aerial photos showing the

results of the bombing. They were somewhat of a consolation to General Bishop, who had been deeply affected by the failure of the main operation. (I'll speak of this setback further on.)

—'Anyway, the defoliants, followed by the napalm and phosphorus, played their role on the trail, as you know. The photos are impressive....'

'Mine aren't bad either,' murmured Madame Ngha. 'But it must be even clearer seen from the sky.'

—'A long denuded corridor more than 200 yards wide can be seen running in an almost continuous line from the Mu-Mok Pass to the edge of hill 873. The precision was such, Colonel Shaw remarked, that the devastation hardly veers from this corridor. It's true: there was no, or almost no, overspill. It almost looks like a road driven through the jungle ...'

'A way,' interrupted Madame Ngha.

—'... a road without a tree or single surviving bush, only burnt ground covered in ash, with scraps of metal jutting out here and there. General Bishop told me that according to numerous experiments their scientists have made and considering the quantity of chemicals discharged, he's positive that not a single plant will grow in this breach for several years....'

'That's good. Kim will be satisfied.'

—'It's a lasting success, he said. No vehicle could take this route now without being spotted immediately. He's very pleased about that. I hope you too are satisfied, dear Aunt Ngha. Then everyone will be happy and my work easier and more fun....'

'Dear Thu,' said Madame Ngha fondly. 'Still her need for that special atmosphere.... But the American scientists are too modest. I have good reason to believe the land will remain clear and sterile for decades. Anyway, go on.'

—'From the wreckage that appeared on the photos, the experts concluded that a large number of tanks and military transports, as well as quite a few field guns, were destroyed, but they couldn't give details. As for the death toll, they hadn't expected to be able to find any way to evaluate it. The general estimates it must have been very high.

—'Only in regard to the main objective did the operation fail, and General Bishop is full of rancour about that. Still, he doesn't have any doubts about the effectiveness of his department, nor does he have the least suspicion as to the real nature of the noises and conversations they picked up. For him, as well as for the entire staff here, this failure was due to bad luck and above all to the poor interpretation of intelligence by the High Command. He's adamant on that point, and I must mention here something of possible importance: I understood from some of his more bitter remarks that a certain distinguished person in General Headquarters had somewhat sarcastically expressed doubts about the adequate functioning of the ears of the jungle. . . .'

'That's bad.'

—'That made the poor general indignant, and he was depressed the whole day.

—'As far as the depots at hill 873 are concerned, I imagine you know as well as I what happened. . . .'

Madame Ngha did know, in fact. When the South Vietnamese, accompanied by American observers, reached their objective, they had indeed found the expected caverns and underground passages, even the three new ones recently fitted out by Giap's order, with their concrete still fresh: but they were all empty. Furthermore, they had been empty for a very long time. Formerly used for storage, they had been abandoned when the traffic was diverted to a different route more than a year before.

Van continued reading: 'General Bishop is still convinced that because of the slow progress of the South Vietnamese, the stores were shifted the week following their initial attack. But there again, at least from what I understood, High Command was astonished that these stocks could have been transferred so quickly if they had been as great as our service reported on the basis of the conversation overheard.

—'Concerning the unexpected arrival of our troops from Laos, I believe the poor general had again been criticized and even accused of negligence, which I find deeply unfair. He himself blames fate and is far from suspecting the truth.

—' "Thu," he said to me plaintively, "those damned thunderstorms prevented us from detecting their approach. What miserable luck, after such a series of happy accidents, I must say...." '

In fact, the troops from the South had no sooner arrived at hill 873 and discovered that the caverns were empty than they were counterattacked by the army from Laos and forced to retreat in disorder. Van went on:

—'The size of that army was also a surprise for the American command, who thought they had wiped out most of the élite troops along the trail. As for General Bishop, he maintains that we had enough reserves to afford to send in two strong contingents on separate fronts. Furthermore, he suspects the authorities of having been misinformed.

—'The only thing left for me to mention is a conversation between Colonel Shaw and General Bishop, which I hope will please you, dear Aunt Ngha. As the latter tried to console himself by recalling what he refers to as the positive side of the operation, that is, the long gap torn out in the mountains, the colonel remarked: "To feel completely at ease, we'd have to carry out the same operation over the entire jungle of the Indochinese peninsula."

—' "Unfortunately that's impossible, my friend," sighed the general. "The total budget of the United States wouldn't cover it. You've no idea how much a raid like the one we just made costs. I discussed it recently with a financial expert. If you added to the actual operation the research work, the laboratories, the factories that had to be built to manufacture truly effective materials, you'd arrive at a fantastic sum, comparable to the budget of a moon landing...." '

'Would you repeat that last phrase, Van?' asked Madame Ngha, stretching her limbs luxuriously like a cat.

With a smile Van obeyed, then continued:

—' "At most we can destroy the jungle along a few particularly dangerous axes. We'll just have to settle for that."

—'That's about all I have to report today, dear Aunt Ngha. . . . No, there's one more detail. The general has put up a large-scale map of Indochina in his office and entrusted me with marking in broad red outline the part that's already been devastated. He likes to keep a graphic representation of the results in front of him and has asked me to update this diagram after each such successful operation, since he seems to be in no doubt that there will be others. It's an easy job and one which interests me.'

After the tender and respectful courtesies Thu always used to end her reports, she added a postscript:

—'The gardener is still at his post and does his work well. We get along fine, and he frequently brings me lovely flowers.'

Madame Ngha raised her head, fixing her gaze on the map of the Indochinese peninsula she had had put up in her office a few days before. It covered practically the entire back wall. Following her instructions, Van had pencilled in two thin parallel lines, representing the great Ho Chi Minh Way proposed by Minister Kim. These lines were imperceptible from a distance, but the sector coloured in red after the first mopping-up operation was strikingly obvious.

She was still absorbed in contemplating this diagram with evident satisfaction when Minister Kim arrived. He too examined the map, first from a distance to judge the whole effect, then up close to see the details. His admiration was evident.

'Extraordinary precision! How did you manage it?'

Indeed, the thick red line hardly deviated from the original pencilled diagram.

'I did see to some of the details,' she replied modestly.

'How wide is it?'

'About two hundred and seventy yards.'

'That's about what we need. Perhaps it will have to be widened slightly, but only in certain places.'

'We can't ask them to do everything,' said Madame Ngha.

'True. Besides, the length is impressive. Close to a hundred miles. It's still not enough, but just the same, not a small proportion of our project.'

'And the length should be ... ?'

'More than twelve hundred miles.'

She sighed.

'Let's hope this will continue. But I'm afraid we won't get the whole thing done.... Still, this already represents some saving.'

'Absolutely. I'll recalculate the estimate and keep it up to date.'

Simply by looking at this first section, which was also one of the most difficult, he was able to calculate that they had saved a considerable amount. She was delighted.

'As a matter of fact, General Bishop has mentioned a very high figure. Do you think it corresponds roughly with your evaluation?'

'You must be joking!' cried Kim. 'His is bound to be much higher. My figure is the minimum compatible with an acceptable result. But they don't bother about expense. I know them well: I've worked for them and with them. As usual, they've overdone it for the sake of their own peace of mind, as well as to spare themselves any long-drawn-out speculations. I've had some samples of the soil taken and analysed by expert chemists. Do you want to know the results? They dropped more than ten times the quantity of chemicals necessary to wipe out everything. For us, that's not so bad; it just makes things more certain.'

Madame Ngha, however, did not seem to be of the same opinion. All of a sudden she frowned, knitting her brows peevishly.

'Do you mean to say,' she asked in an impatient voice, 'that with the same quantity they could have treated an area ten times larger?'

'That's exactly what I meant.'

'Wastrels!' she cried, pursing her lips in irritation.

8

That evening General Bishop, in a state of unaccustomed agitation, arrived at his office later than usual. It was already dark and Thu was at her post. He passed hurriedly through the monitoring room without pausing to make his habitual inspection or ask even a single question; indeed, he scarcely responded to the greeting of his secretary, who had risen as he entered—he who was always so polite to her. Without a word he sat down, called for Colonel Shaw, and abruptly demanded: 'Shaw, send the week's duty officer to me immediately. And you can tell him not to be expecting any congratulations.'

Encountering such a grim mood, Shaw asked no questions and hastily disappeared. The general then offered Thu a word of apology for his rudeness and, feeling the need to explain, said: 'I'm furious. It's that gardener's fault, that Javanese. I regret it now, but I almost hit him.'

'The gardener? What has he done, sir?'

Had the general been at all in possession of his senses he might have noticed his secretary shudder, but he was too beside himself to pay the least attention.

'What did he do? Listen, Thu, I caught him . . .'

But she was forced to wait a few moments before learning the reason for his agitation. The duty officer presented himself and, forewarned by Shaw, displayed in exemplary fashion every mark of respect due to his superior officer. He was a young lieutenant responsible for the proper day-to-day running of the centre for the week, a duty each of the junior officers took in turn, which included seeing to the mess, the kitchens, and the upkeep of the bungalows.

The general at once reassumed his gruffest manner.

'Would you like to know what I came across today, Hudson?'

The lieutenant's expression made it obvious he did not.

'Well, I'll tell you: I saw our gardener, *my* gardener, spraying my gravel with *weed killer*.'

'Sir,' stammered the young man, 'I had no idea. . . .'

'You should have,' said the general icily. 'It's part of your duty. But that's not all. . . .'

This was a period when the civilized world, and especially the United States, was seized by a fever of anxiety and indignation at the idea that mankind, in its disregard for the environment, was everywhere committing unnatural crimes whose already tragic consequences threatened to transform the biosphere, within a very short period, according to some specialists, into a nauseous ooze, where all life would be impossible.

Though isolated and plunged into a world it found confusing, the American army of the Far East kept in touch with its own country through a permanent network of communications, in particular by tons of newspapers delivered each day by plane that contained page after page of comment on pollution and preached the urgency of a relentless crusade against this sacrilege. The army could hardly fail to be infected by this sudden fever. While the raids of total destruction continued over the Ho Chi Minh Trail, less intensively than at first but still at a pace restrained only by delays in producing the ingredients and by the enormity of the burden it imposed on the national defence budget, General Bishop, won over to the cause from the very beginning, acquainted himself each day with new details of this plague that threatened the world, and took careful note of the measures recommended for averting it, waxing indignant whenever he sensed the least indifference towards this problem in those around him.

This is why the discovery he had just made so outraged him that he was still shaking with fury. The incident had occurred in the garden of the bungalow he occupied not far from the monitoring room, a small garden, but carefully maintained like the others by the Javanese, Sutan. The general often relaxed there with a whisky before going to his office in the evening, enjoying the peace that reigned over this part of Thailand when the neighbouring B-52's were not taking off. That is what he had intended to do this particular night. He had been heading towards a little, finely gravelled patch in front of his veranda, just beside a small lawn, when he found his armchair shifted and the gardener absorbed in what seemed to him to be a very peculiar occupation. Squatting, with a tiny watering can in his hand similar to those used by city dwellers with a somewhat bucolic bent to sprinkle the three pots of flowers on their balconies, Sutan was parsimoniously and methodically spreading a liquid on the gravel, several drops to the square inch. The thought of using such an instrument for watering had offended the general's Taylorism, and led him to ask: 'Don't you have a bigger watering can with your tools?'

The Javanese had laughed heartily and stood up. He really was a gardener and knew his job, apart from his duties in Madame Ngha's service. He showed the officer the contents of the can. It was a greenish liquid, obviously not pure water. The general's face had clouded as he began to suspect some perverse assault on nature.

'What's that?' he had asked.

He still trembled with fury as he described the scene to the duty officer: 'Then do you know what this brute showed me?'

The gardener, still laughing, had put under his nose a package bearing the brand name of a common weed killer.

He had tried to explain that the contents of this little watering can would be enough to keep the gravel clear for several months. But by then the general was far too worked up to admit even the least explanation.

'After that I rushed to the hut where this character keeps his tools, figuring he might be trying to conceal some other poisons there. And would you like to know what else I found?'

He had to describe the scene in every detail, both to justify his indignation and to make the lieutenant share in it. Again Thu was worried. She knew Sutan sometimes kept a message from Madame Ngha in this hut before getting a chance to deliver it.

It was soon apparent, however, that the general's mind was a million miles from espionage. Even if there had been a suspicious message in the hut, he would never have noticed it. He paused, carefully timing his effect like a clever actor out to impress his audience then hammered out his words as he slammed his fist on the table: 'I found a half-empty sack of DDT! I said: DDT, Hudson!'

Thu heaved a sigh of relief. But not the young officer, who blushed in confusion.

'Sir,' he stammered, 'I ...'

He tried to explain that it was standard practice on all the installations to spread a little DDT around the houses every night to lower the risk of malaria. But since the general disapproved, he would take immediate steps to put a stop to it, and the order would be passed on to the next duty officer. He promised these acts of vandalism would not be repeated.

'Very well,' approved the general, beginning to calm down.

'But we still have the problem of the mosquitoes, sir,' the young man added courageously. 'Maybe we could keep them from reproducing by spreading a little kerosene in the ditches around here.'

'Kerosene!'

'It was the method used by the old colonialists, sir, before DDT even existed.'

'Kerosene!'

The general seemed on the verge of another fit of rage. Nevertheless, with a violent effort he mastered himself and, when he had managed to calm down, said to the lieutenant in a paternal though authoritarian tone: 'Listen here, Hudson. I don't think you've understood me clearly. Take a look at this.'

Out of a drawer he pulled a pile of newspaper clippings, documentation on the nature and consequences of pollution that he had patiently amassed day after day for weeks. Certain passages had been marked in red, sometimes with three or four impassioned strokes. The young officer was granted a long lecture full of examples on the ill wrought by chemicals that not only despoiled nature, rotting it like a pestilence, but also accumulated in the bodies of animals and eventually man through the intermediary of the vegetation. He learned that kerosene, if not as pernicious as DDT, must still be severely proscribed, since most of the waterways were already infected with it, and rivers and underground streams ultimately reach the sea, where these noxious agents gradually accumulate, destroying the algae, plankton and fish, and transforming our oceans into cesspools.

He carried on like this for some time, receiving an occasional tender glance from Thu, who now felt reassured. When he had finished, he checked whether the lieutenant had understood the lesson by asking several questions, then sent him away with precise instructions for the future, determined to safeguard the integrity of the environment, at least here, where final responsibility was his.

General Bishop was not the only officer in Thailand or Vietnam to be preoccupied with the environment. This issue, no doubt aggravated by the tropical sun, provoked in some a peculiar mental derangement that at times reached the heights of sublime folly.

One remarkable example was provided by a colonel who

commanded an armoured regiment during an attack in Cambodia. Having surrounded a group of hamlets in which guerrillas were hiding, he had received the order to begin the final assault with his tanks, armed to the teeth with cannon firing napalm and phosphorous shells, when suddenly, just as the vehicles set off with a thunderous roar, the colonel behaved in a most surprising way.

He rushed onto the battlefield, gesticulating furiously and shouting frantic commands. When he at last made himself heard, it was understood he was ordering all the tanks to stop their engines immediately and remain in position. Despite some astonishment, this was done. Then, disregarding the entreaties of a sympathetic chief of staff, who tried in vain to dissuade him, he sent a succession of vehement cables to General Headquarters, demanding that they at once send a team of specialized mechanics, capable (he considered his were not) of correctly adjusting the carburettors of the armoured vehicles. He was no novice and remembered the courses in mechanics he had taken in his youth. When he had seen the heavy black fumes belching from the exhausts and smelled the stench that already hung over the plain where the attack was to take place, he had realized that these carburettors were badly adjusted, like those of the automobiles cruising around New York and Los Angeles, and that since the combustion was incomplete, they were sending into the earth's atmosphere great quantities of poisonous gases, which he enumerated one by one to his dumbfounded subordinates.

A further remarkable aspect of this incident was that the High Command had not immediately understood the nature of the sickness that had overcome the colonel. Since his anticipated retirement came only a few weeks later, by which time he had given still more striking proof of his mental aberration, they had thought that the dispatch of these specialists must be indispensable to the pursuit of the operation, and had promptly sent the requested team of mechanics.

These were highly qualified men. In less than forty-eight

hours they had adjusted the carburettors in such a way that the pollution was limited to a reasonable level. After a few tries the colonel announced himself satisfied and finally gave the order to attack. The suspect hamlets were wiped out by fire and steel with a delay of only two days.

9

Meanwhile, after its birth in the heads of a few crackpots and having first fluttered through the silent and obscure layers of the population, the idea that biological warfare might after all constitute an act of pollution and an assault on the environment finally crossed the minds of a few important Americans. It took several more months for that suspicion to succeed in penetrating the thick walls of the Pentagon, but when it did it proliferated there, exciting feverish reactions, passionate discussions, and even some loss of sleep.

Following its own course up the hierarchy, this idea came to occupy the White House. Once there, passed along by a gang of advisers and experts of every variety, it eventually nestled in the President's office, where it installed itself for good, impossible to dislodge. The President had only one way to rid himself of it: to declare the end of Biological Warfare and return to the good old days of saturation bombing with conventional explosives, which had less pernicious, or in any case less durable, effects on the environment.

Having taken that decision, the President permitted a delay of a few months to liquidate stores and to some extent amortize the huge expense of a tactic that had turned out to be a very bad financial proposition, even though the military had figured it would pay. This reprieve somewhat comforted Madame Ngha and the Minister of Construction, both of whom were deeply grieved by this untimely decision just at the moment when their plan was so well on its way to completion.

It was the anniversary of the operation at hill 873, the symbolic ground-breaking on the gigantic site of the triumphal way. Kim and Madame Ngha made a rough assessment of the work's progress.

Week after week it had steadily advanced, allowing the addition from time to time of another fraction of the red line on the diagram. Manipulating the ears of the jungle had become a familiar routine, as had the shifting of the wreckage from one section of the trail to another after it had served to demonstrate the effectiveness of each raid on the enemy observers' photographs.

Both stood deep in contemplation before the large map and followed Van's performance with great interest. She was busy bringing the red line up to date with the results of the latest operation.

Perched upon a stool, Van had first outlined in pencil the section torn from the jungle's grasp a few days earlier. She came down from her perch to pick up a fine brush and tiny pot of red ink, then climbed back up to finish her task with meticulous care, her glasses glued to the map to avoid making any smudges. When she had finished she moved back a bit to judge the effect. Madame Ngha exchanged a glance with Kim and sighed. The morning's addition was limited to a little dot, distinguishable only by the still fresh ink that shone in contrast to the previous line. It was barely a twenty-fifth of an inch long. At most a few dozen yards on the ground.

'Even so,' remarked Kim on a note of optimism, 'a few inches here and there, all adds up to quite a respectable result after a year.'

'Maybe. But at the present rate, since they have been decreasing their efforts regularly for several weeks now, we would need at least two or three years to finish. And we don't even have one. I'm sure of that.'

'But the Way is not the only thing. The main centres are already well advanced.'

As usual she was difficult to satisfy. But after another glance at the map, while Van was putting the stool and utensils away, she admitted the results could have been worse.

There were, to begin with, quite a few rather long continuous red lines. The main one connected the Mu-Mok Pass with hill 873, that first triumph whose size and perfection were as yet unequalled. Another almost unbroken section in the south followed the Cambodian border, while farther north there was a third section at the conjunction of the three frontiers. Two more, smaller, one of which went on towards Laos and the other towards Cambodia perpendicular to the great north-south axis, sketched a united Vietnam's future connections with its neighbours.

In other sectors the red line was far from being continuous. A good part of the diagram was made up of uneven dashes, sporadic periods, and the occasional modest hyphen of a quarter of an inch or so. Some of these were separated here and there by large empty spaces, making it difficult for the eye to follow the line that should have joined them. Madame Ngha stared at these chasms and sighed again, muttering a few words of apology, as if feeling the need to justify them.

'It hasn't always been possible to lead them to the desired spot.'

'But look,' interrupted Kim with a shrug.

He picked up a bamboo rod and pointed out a dot at the intersection of two lines, which looked like a large, bright piece of confetti.

'Here is the site for our model mountain resort, which

will be named after Ho Chi Minh, where we needed a broad surface area as well as a longitudinal opening. And there it is—exactly where it should be. So that's been achieved.'

'That's true,' she admitted. 'Less than two months ago. I think it might be considered a rather fine success.'

'An achievement very much to the credit of your department.'

She deigned a smile and assumed an air of modesty.

'We were lucky. The enemy was planning to use a vast number of helicopters and paratroops in a new ground attack against our trail. That had nothing to do with me ... or almost nothing. Still, such a concentration required a large landing area. Thu gave me plenty of warning, and where we did display some ingenuity was in guiding them to that precise point. Anyway, it's been done and I'm not unhappy with the results. Judging from the plans you showed me, I think the area cleared will be adequate for our model resort; there will be enough space to build your projected bungalows and hotels so that you can put up a reasonable contingent of holidaymakers and tourists. I know that area. The air is deliciously pure. I have to admit your plan appealed to me, and I did everything I could to achieve it.

'And here,' continued the Minister, deliberately optimistic that morning as he pointed out a lone red rectangle, 'will be the future atomic power centre we've decided to construct close to the junction of the three borders, permitting us to distribute energy not only to our own region but to Cambodia and Laos as well, and even as far as Thailand, if she asks for it. That too has been finished.'

'Or at least the ground prepared. A good ten or twelve acres. You're right, Kim, it's not negligible.'

They went on taking objective stock of the situation and establishing some order of priority for future operations. This to her was essential.

'For according to the latest declarations of the American

President,' she said, 'we have no more than a few months in which to count on their collaboration. That means working at twice the speed.'

5

WREATH OF ORCHIDS

I

Madame Ngha had asked Kim if he would call by her office
so that she could give him some information she thought
might interest him. It was contained in Thu's last report,
and she read him this passage:

—'As you must know, defoliants are now forbidden. Pro-
duction has been stopped and the last stocks were dropped
in a heavy raid a few days ago. At least I think that's correct
since it was General Bishop who confided it to me. He hardly
keeps any secrets from me now. I was able to add one more
fairly long line to the map, but I'm afraid it's the last....'

'That's it, Kim,' said Madame Ngha with a touch of nostalgia, 'it's all over, for you too, Van: this is the last time
you'll carry out your little task.'

Perched up on the stool, her secretary was in the process
of tracing a segment in red, thus removing an unpleasant-
looking gap. Though not completely covered in red, at least
the original pencilled diagram was now marked out by
enough dots and lines for the skeleton of the Ho Chi Minh
Way to emerge if the map were viewed from a distance.
They all succumbed to the melancholy that hovers gloomily
over the end of a glorious epoch.

'After all, it couldn't last forever,' said Kim. 'And they
never caught on that it was a fraud?'

'No, at least not Service S. But listen to this:

—'No one here suspected your plan. General Bishop
simply made a few sarcastic remarks about our obstinacy in
almost always having the convoys follow the same course,
regardless of the frequency and violence of the attacks. He
came to the conclusion that the enemy was presenting them

with a challenge, and that such blind pride would in the end lead to their ruin. . . .'

'Pride . . .' commented Madame Ngha thoughtfully. 'But I know they're now having serious doubts about the effectiveness of the ears of the jungle at General Headquarters, Kim, and certain passages in the report confirm it. Though that wouldn't interest you.'

'Anyway, it's hardly of much importance now that the major operations are over.'

She hesitated slightly, as if she did not completely agree with this last remark, then nodded and read another phrase:

—'Therefore, the bombings will resume with conventional explosives. . . .'

'But that's extremely irritating,' interrupted the Minister. 'Conventional explosives, as your agent put it, produce craters, sometimes very deep ones. They're going to sabotage our highway.'

'From now on not a single engine will be heard along this route,' replied Madame Ngha. 'Orders have already been given. It must be completely abandoned by the convoys. They will think we've at last understood it's too dangerous and assume that prudence has finally got the better of our pride.'

She read out a few more sentences she thought might interest Kim, and then folded up the report. The rest of the document did not concern him, though it contained information she considered important. Only after the Minister had departed did she read over certain passages with Van, the one person who was in on all her secrets.

—'Following your last instructions, the gardener brings a large bouquet of flowers every week for the general, who adores them and is absolutely delighted. Sutan is therefore back in his good graces and the affair of the weed killer forgotten. The general has put me in charge of arranging the flowers in his living room. He says I'm the only one who knows how to do it properly. I'm very flattered. . . .'

146

Madame Ngha was reading half-aloud, more to herself than to Van. She then paused for a moment, lost in a dream, and her secretary took the opportunity to make an observation.

'I noticed you've underlined this passage.'

'Underlined, did I? ... Oh, you're right.'

'Thu seems very proud of the general's compliments. But I don't exactly see what benefit that is to us.'

'I don't either,' said Madame Ngha, recovering herself. 'I certainly must have been up in the clouds.'

Van looked at her suspiciously, but Madame Ngha began reading again.

—'I now have to report some news that will undoubtedly annoy you. I believe our department's days are numbered, and perhaps also the period of General Bishop's active service. Anyway, that's the rumour circulating among the staff. He hasn't said anything specific to me, but he's been going around for several days with a sad expression that's very disturbing. Since he's implied that he soon expects to have more time to devote to writing his book, I think there must be some truth in it.

—'At any rate, I know from a reliable source (a confidential memo I managed to read) that Headquarters is beginning to distrust the intelligence provided by the ears of the jungle, and beyond that, the way in which it is being interpreted by the general. I think I'll be sorry if he goes—primarily, of course, because of the immense services he has rendered our cause, but also because I'm sure he himself is not wicked. He has always behaved properly, even paternally towards me. Once he intervened to put some young officer who was pestering me in his place; he did it so well that now all the staff is very respectful and most considerate to me. But perhaps there's no need to report all this....'

'Good girl, Thu,' commented Madame Ngha.

'Don't you think it's about time her service ended as well? It seems as if she's beginning to feel a little too comfortable there.'

'We've talked about that before, Van,' said Madame Ngha gravely, 'and there's nothing to add to what I've already said. I don't see anything wrong with Thu's feeling comfortable in Thailand, or even in her being susceptible to certain attentions.... You can rest assured,' she added somewhat dryly, 'I know how to choose my agents for the missions I want them to carry out. Thu is perfectly placed and will perform her duty to the end.'

—'For the moment, the department is still functioning more or less normally, but it's all become a sort of routine. There's a feeling of boredom, and the dedication and enthusiasm of the beginning have completely disappeared. Headquarters' suspicions, and the dissatisfaction they've shown, seem to have dampened morale. Colonel Shaw is practically the only one who still shows a bit of excitement from time to time, but only when he's succeeded in capturing the screech of some rare insect.

—'The general too has let himself be overcome by this inertia. When the sounds of trucks are sent in to him he hardly even glances at the screen. He just pushes the buttons and pays no further attention to the activity carried on by the computers....'

She paused again, apparently absorbed in a dream, which this time Van dared not interrupt. Suddenly Madame Ngha asked: 'Didn't anything in this passage strike you?'

'I noticed that you underlined the last sentence.'

'Do you have any idea why?'

Van thought for a moment, then had to confess ignorance.

'Neither do I. I must have been totally absent-minded when I read this report. Still, there must have been a good reason.'

—'... he hardly even glances at the screen. He just pushes the buttons and pays no further attention to the activity carried on by the computers....'

She pondered, her forehead creased, then continued in a firmer tone:

'She's written the "computers". *Plural*, Van. That must

mean, first of all, the huge IBM in Thailand that records the signals, calculates the coordinates of the ears that are transmitting, and relays the information to the F-4's; and second, the computers in the aircraft receiving this data.'

'No doubt.'

'Now listen to this.'

Her attitude had changed, and with it her gaze. It now appeared focused on a precise point discernible only to her, but the brilliance of which was undoubtedly what made her eyes sparkle with the radiance that occasionally earned her the nickname 'Shimmering Light'. She took a paper from her desk and read.

'Listen carefully: "The F-4 pilots then feed this information into their own aircraft computers and fly direct to the target with no need for further navigation. In the event the weather is bad, the computers will make an automatic release of weapons at the proper point.... The only drawback, airmen say, is that they must wait for reconnaissance in better weather to determine how successful the attack was." '*

'Do you know where I found that?'

'Most likely in another agent's report that you've kept secret even from me,' said Van almost resentfully.

'Not at all. It's published in the American *Armed Forces Journal*, which is available to anyone. I read it regularly. ... So, you see: frequently, and always if the weather is bad, the pilots themselves don't interfere. It's the computers that direct the aircraft and launch the bombardment at the proper moment.'

Another silence. But this time she was not dreaming. She was deep in thought.

'The weather is very often foggy at this time of year,' she resumed in a mild voice, 'foggy over Vietnam, and over Thailand as well.... On top of that, according to Thu's information, there's no longer any enthusiasm among the

* *Armed Forces Journal*, February 15, 1971.

monitoring staff. She spoke of disenchantment and routine. It's just possible that this state of mind has overwhelmed all those participating in these operations, including the F-4 pilots. What do you think of that supposition, Van?'

'It seems perfectly reasonable to me. All the information we have tends to indicate that enemy morale is low among the ground troops as well as the pilots.'

'Do you think it would be possible to make a synthesis of everything we've just said?'

She now spoke with unusual animation. Van knew from certain familiar signs that a brilliant scheme was being hatched out in her boss's brain. She thought for a moment, then said modestly:

'As far as I can see, these's nothing really new, but I believe the situation could be summed up in this way: the sound picked up by an ear of the jungle acts as a trigger, launching a raid and fatally attracting the bombs onto the ear itself.'

Madame Ngha regarded her secretary with admiration.

'That's exactly it,' she approved, 'you've chosen the perfect word. "Fatally" is just what I was looking for.'

Van blushed with pleasure and continued to stare at Madame Ngha, who, looking her straight in the eyes, expressed herself with careful deliberation.

'General Bishop and his staff have rendered us valuable services, no?'

'Certainly.'

'But judging from Thu's last report, it seems they can no longer be of any use to us. Don't you agree?'

Van nodded once more. She sensed these remarks were leading up to some logically unassailable conclusion that she felt she was just beginning to discern. But Madame Ngha did not seem to have anything to add for the moment. It was unlike her to bluntly state the outcome of an analysis that would be obvious to an acute mind from a few mere allusions. And such was the case: any further comment would have seemed to her to defile the beauty of the scheme she had just glimpsed. As she remained silent, almost ready to fall back into her reverie, Van, her curiosity aroused, ventured to revive the conversation.

'Have you discovered some important point in the report that might have escaped me, Madame?'

'What? ... No; nothing very important, other than Thu's asking for instructions in the event that Service S is abolished. She would probably be transferred. Saigon or somewhere else.... She also appears to be rather distressed. I imagine she's not particularly enthusiastic about playing the role she performed so well beside General Bishop in some other office. It would probably be better if she were to come back here with us. I'll have to give it more thought.'

'Then you consider her job there is finished?' asked Van, slightly astonished.

'That's not exactly what I was thinking,' said Madame Ngha with a smile. 'On the contrary, I believe she can render us one last, extremely important service. After that I'll organize her escape and arrange for her return.'

Considering the conversation over, she got up and took her cap from the bamboo peg, putting it on as she prepared to leave the office. Just at the doorstep, however, she made a final remark.

'The monitoring centre in Thailand is composed of a large and, more important, highly qualified staff: physicists, engineers, men of inestimable value to our enemy. If the results haven't been all they anticipated, it's not their fault, but the military's, which has made poor use of them.'

'And a little bit ours too,' Van observed.

'Right. But some other time they could easily perfect an invention as ingenious as the ears of the jungle, which might well do us a great deal of harm. Don't you think so, Van?'

'Obviously,' replied her secretary.

Then after a few seconds' reflection, as she modestly lowered the thick glasses that gave her the air of a provincial school mistress, she added: 'Nor must we forget that Service S is very close to the B-52 base.'

'I am more and more satisfied with our collaboration, Van,' cried Madame Ngha. 'It's always a pleasure to talk with you. I like it when someone picks up my hints.... You know, I wonder if old Ami's spirits haven't inspired us both today.'

Van pushed her glasses back and stared at her boss, whose regular features were at this moment distorted by a broad smile. Madame Ngha had nothing to add, however, and stuffing a lock of hair back into her cap, left the office with a friendly wave. She did not hear the quiet reply of her secretary as she leaned over her desk stacked with papers.

'If it's not the Westerner's Devil.'

2

Thu was right when she characterized General Bishop's attitude towards her as paternal. From their first meeting he had been moved by this slender shadow with the face of a sombre child, whose eyes were often veiled in a mist of melancholy. Dressed in an inappropriate uniform, its sole ornament a ribbon of white silk, symbol of her mourning, she presented a touching and dissonant figure in this department of engineers. He had been divorced for some time and rarely saw his own daughter; on those few occasions when he did he felt like a stranger, disconcerted by her casual manner. He retained a painful memory of their last meeting. With Thu, however, he felt at ease. He liked her reserve and discretion, qualities he appreciated in the young.

He had taken an interest in her, lending her books and frequently inviting her for tea in his bungalow. Yet this familiarity never aroused gossip, since it was so strikingly obvious to his subordinates that General Bishop was incapable of harbouring any unscrupulous designs. He took pleasure in hearing her recount stories about her country and the memories of her childhood in her now irreproachable English, which still kept its inimitable Vietnamese lilt. He had been moved to tears as she related the tragedy that had left her alone in the world.

She told of having lost her parents and two brothers in a savage attack by the Vietcong. It was the massacre of her family that had later motivated her voluntary enlistment in the American army. This story, formerly attested to by statements from local dignitaries, deviated from the truth only in its details: her entire family had indeed perished, but during a bombing by American B-52's. Still, having repeated her story innumerable times to the authorities who had investigated her, she now related it to the general without the least restraint, and derived some consolation from the compassion he showed her.

She was grateful to him, as she had faithfully reported to Madame Ngha, for doing everything possible to ease her difficult position, that of a young Vietnamese girl alone on a base in Thailand, among soldiers and American officers who, even if not generally behaving as they did in conquered countries, still had a naïve, deep-seated feeling of superiority over the Asians in every sphere. Thu's sensitive nature appreciated General Bishop's tact and good breeding, in particular the fact that he had always considered her a child and treated her as such, never attempting even the slightest flirtation, in contrast to what had happened in other branches of the army where she had worked in the past, leaving her with memories as painful as those of her experiences with the Vietcong commandos. On the contrary, she had felt it her duty to inform Madame Ngha—as a diligent agent always gives information of a psychological nature that might prove useful—that as far as this matter was concerned, the general had given strict orders for her youth to be respected and had intervened with an authority he was sometimes capable of exhibiting to protect her from the advances of a young offi-

153

cer. First, he had reprimanded him curtly and then, reminding him of the obligations of military honour, had lectured him with such severity that the poor wretch felt guilty of an unnatural crime, and presented his most humble apologies to the young girl. After that no one in Service S dared make a compromising gesture or remark.

In return she rendered services that simplified the general's solitary existence. She acted as a kind of housekeeper in the bungalow he occupied and spent several hours each day checking the linen and seeing that there were always some vases of his favourite flowers arranged tastefully around the rooms.

All this had created bonds between them, bonds that were almost familial. It was a friendship tinged with tenderness on his part; she had become a glimmer of sunshine in his isolation, here in a Thailand where he often felt like an intruder and was surrounded by a staff whose scientific preoccupations were utterly foreign to him. He was grateful for the human touch she had brought into his existence, a touch almost poetic at times, which had become indispensable and allowed him to resist the debilitating climate and dreariness of exile without having to resort, as some did, to excessive drinking or the use of other drugs.

As for her, the feelings she had towards General Bishop were mixed with a certain perplexity, often expressed in an ambiguous wrinkle of her delicate nose, which could just as easily have been interpreted as scorn for the attentions of some stray dog as the amazed gratitude she felt at seeing herself treated with such kindness.

That night she had already completed her housekeeping chores and finished straightening up the bungalow when the general invited her to have a cup of tea on the veranda. He was just finishing his whiskey before going to the office, as he had done at this hour for years. Despite his present disenchantment, he continued to carry out his duties punctually and stayed almost every night until two in the morning.

He was particularly depressed, and for reasons having little to do with the gloomy weather enveloping Thailand that night. An official message had arrived that morning notifying him of the suspension of Service S. The army of technicians would return to Saigon the following week, where they were to be reorganized on a new basis and under a new command. The message also mentioned that General Bishop should prepare to receive a new assignment. Another message, this time confidential, specified the assignment as retirement. About this last point the general had not told anyone except Thu, to whom he had recently permitted himself to confide his sense of frustration and humiliation.

For a moment he contemplated the sky over Thailand, where heavy clouds were piling up. He then turned his eyes on the young girl.

'Tonight will be our last night monitoring the jungle,' he said bitterly. 'Tomorrow the service is to stop all activity.'

'The last night!'

Thu trembled and twirled the spoon in her teacup nervously, looking around anxiously as if expecting and at the same time fearing something ominous from outside. The general noticed this and put her attitude down to the same melancholy he himself felt. He tried to console her.

'Don't worry, Thu. You'll find another post in some congenial department.'

Then, after a silence, he let out his resentment.

'Incredible,' he said. 'Our service should have been considered one of the most precious sources of information. We've had brilliant successes. How many trucks have been destroyed thanks to us! How many tons of munitions wiped out!'

'It's impossible to estimate, sir, but certainly a considerable number.'

'Well, they're not satisfied. They're pretending there have never been so many convoys on the Ho Chi Minh Trail. In so many words they're accusing me of incompetence, even negligence.'

'It's shameful,' cried Thu with a sincerity that went straight to his heart.

'We'll have to leave this part of Thailand, and just when I was beginning to get used to it. It's so peaceful here.'

'Yes,' agreed Thu.

Then, with a trace of her mournful grimace, she added thoughtfully: 'At least when the B-52's aren't taking off.'

'I'm going to devote myself to my book. As for you, Thu, you'll be sent somewhere else. Do you have any preference? Would you like to stay in Thailand? Another post could easily be found for you here. Or would you prefer to go back to your own country? The situation in the south has improved now. If I still have any credibility left, I could try to get you the assignment you wanted.'

Rather paradoxically, Thu also felt her heart contract at the thought of leaving this place, especially her bungalow, where each night the familiar shadows responded to her greeting.

'I don't want to go back to Vietnam.'

'Poor child,' murmured the general, placing his hand paternally on her shoulder. 'I understand. Too many bitter memories. But think it over some more, and tell me what you've decided in the morning.'

But he noticed she was not listening any longer. Her gaze was fixed on a point behind the hedge enclosing the garden. In the premature twilight created over Thailand by the fog, the general glimpsed a shadow passing through the gate and quickly recognized the Javanese gardener.

'It's only old Sutan,' he said with a smile to reassure Thu, in whose eyes he had caught a flash of panic.

The gardener approached timidly. He stopped in front of the veranda and bowed.

'What is it, Sutan?'

'I wanted to bring you these flowers tonight, sir. They're very rare. My brother found them in the forest.'

He held out his arms and presented a large bouquet of delicately tinted orchids, magnificent flowers and rare indeed, though they could sometimes be found in the depths of the tropical jungle.

3

'Good man,' said General Bishop. 'And to think, Thu, I once nearly beat him!'

He thanked him with genuine emotion. At this critical moment of his career, the slightest consideration moved him deeply.

Thu remained silent and absolutely still, teacup in hand, her eyes staring straight at the orchids the man held out, as if she were the victim of a strange hypnosis. Surprised by her behaviour, since tending to the flowers was one of her duties, the general himself had begun to move awkwardly forward to receive the gift when she at last came out of her trance and, quickly forestalling him, grasped the bunch of flowers, their stems wrapped in moss that smelled of the musty jungle.

'I'll take care of them, sir. . . . They're splendid.'

'Splendid,' agreed the general. 'At home you never see any as beautiful as this. Only the jungles of the Far East produce such pearls.'

Thu and Sutan exchanged a furtive glance while the general bent over the flowers and breathed in their aroma with pleasure, cheered as much by their beauty as by the humble gardener's touching gesture. He thanked him again and insisted on giving him a princely tip, which the gardener, after profuse objections, finally accepted. Then, having bowed once more, the Javanese turned on his heels and vanished into the darkness.

Thu and the general returned to the living room. Before switching on the light, he carefully closed the glass door to keep out the mosquitoes that, since they were no longer combated, had begun to invade the centre in earnest. A pool of light flooded the garden, illuminating the gardener's cap as he disappeared behind the hedge.

'They're good people,' the general murmured again thoughtfully. 'All you have to do is treat them well and they become quite attached to you.'

He shook his head, suddenly depressed at the thought of going back to the office that, under the present circumstances, had become pure drudgery.

'I'll have to go, Thu,' he said, rising ponderously. 'I'd never forgive myself if I wasn't at my post on the last night. Would you lock up the bungalow and bring me the keys?'

The Thai servant who did the cleaning had already left for the barracks some distance away where the domestics slept. He would only return in the morning, in time to prepare coffee.

'All right, sir. I'll put these cups away and arrange the flowers.'

'Thank you, Thu. I wonder how I'll ever manage without you.... But speaking of these flowers, there are quite a few—far too many for me. I'd like you to take half of them home with you.'

'Thank you, sir,' she said, obviously affected by his thoughtfulness. 'I'll do as you say.'

'See you later, then. You may as well take your time over dinner, and not rush to get back to the office. There's no point in killing yourself with work when what we're doing doesn't seem to amount to anything.'

As he was about to leave her with these bitter words, which summed up all his lassitude and humiliation, he felt a sudden burst of energy and raised his head.

158

'After all, who knows if this last night might not give us a chance to distinguish ourselves.'

'Of course, sir,' she cried with unaffected spontaneity, so much did she hate seeing him dejected. 'We must never lose hope.'

'A chance to strike a terrific blow against the enemy, with results that would be confirmed tomorrow and dumbfound all our detractors,' continued the general, clenching his fists.

'I'll pray for it, sir; I promise.'

So, his spirits somewhat restored, General Bishop left his bungalow and headed towards the monitoring room with a lighter step. He always went on foot: it was only a couple of hundred yards away.

A few moments after he had left, Thu silently opened the door and, paying no heed to the mosquitoes, listened. When the sound of his footsteps had died away she carefully closed it again and for a while stood quiet and pensive in the sudden, eerie silence of the bungalow, her face tense, a faraway look in her eyes. Then, as if shattering a dream, she awoke and approached the bouquet of orchids she had put on the table, slowly beginning to unwrap the newspaper around the base of the stems. Her long tapered fingers probed the moss and froze at the touch of a hard object. She grimaced—for a second her features expressed the same horror as when the B-52's took off. She placed the orchids back on the table and moved away with obvious revulsion.

She put the bungalow in order as she had promised the general, replacing the bottle of whiskey in the bar, putting the glass and tea service on a tray, and carrying them all into the kitchen, where she washed them herself. This domestic ritual was performed with precise, unconscious movements, betraying a deep inner preoccupation. With the same mechanical gestures she put away the dishes, switched off the light, and returned to the living room, where she stopped in front of the table and with the same distracted air allowed herself a moment's anxious contemplation, as if unable to make up her mind to touch the orchids. Still, there was a faint gleam in her eye as she reflected that these were the loveliest flowers in the world.

The general reached the monitoring room and forced himself to adopt an air of unconcern before the staff. He made his usual rounds and addressed a few words to each of the technicians, asking if there was anything new. Their replies were all much the same: the only sounds this evening were the eternal night bird, the murmur of running water, and the chirping of a few crickets. No sign of any suspicious human activity.

He finished his rounds and entered his office, having advised everyone to redouble their vigilance. Alone, he again felt a surge of anger at the lack of comprehension and the presumptuousness of Headquarters. The mad hope that had seized him a moment before returned. If only he could shut them up! Surrender his duties, maybe, but only after a master stroke! Some brilliant exploit, with incontestable results, before which the bureaucrats would be forced to submit and make proper amends. At this manly thought, he again clenched his fists: it helped him rise above the bleakness of his solitude.

4

The orchids fully deserved Thu's fervent admiration; they were indeed the most beautiful flowers in the world. That had been Madame Ngha's intention, perhaps because her keen mind, sensitive to even the most imperceptible nuances of human behaviour, foresaw that Thu's task would thus be made easier, or perhaps because an aesthetic impulse prompted her to place her magnificently conceived plan in a setting worthy of it.

When she had left Van, after what she considered a fruitful conversation, she had gone to find Dr. Wang, who became so fascinated at the mere suggestion of her plan that he happily abandoned the delicate experiment he was performing in his laboratory and at once rushed back to his office with her, where they closeted themselves.

The two collaborators conferred for more than an hour, the Chinese scientist examining the technical side of the problem while she gave him all the details in her possession on the nature of the objective and the layout of the locale. The initial result of their exchange was to decide definitely on a bouquet of flowers as the most propitious agent of destiny. This had been in the back of her mind since the earliest stages of her scheme, but she was pleased to find that the conclusion of Dr. Wang's scientific analysis matched her own intuition. Not only was there no technical contingency prohibiting the use of flowers, but quite the contrary, they lent themselves admirably to the project.

It only remained to choose the kind of flower. At this point Dr. Wang sent for one of his colleagues, a young man in whom he placed great hopes, who specialized in industrial design and possessed a good knowledge of electronics as well as being an artist. Once acquainted with the project and what was expected of him, this expert scarcely hesitated before giving his opinion, asserting that to him it was obvious that the orchid had been created for all eternity to play the specific role the flowers had been assigned. Madame Ngha reacted to his statement in a manner most startling for a secret-service chief. As if catapulted, she leapt from her seat and on one of those impulses that were in such direct contrast to her usual reserve and high office—though they provided one of the more pungent aspects of her character—flung herself upon the young man, kissing him on both cheeks and clasping him to her breast. Again she was right. From the outset her intuition had fixed on no other flower than the orchid. Her unusual behaviour could be accounted for not only by her delight at having her instinctive clairvoyance confirmed, but also by the exhilaration she had felt for hours because of the shimmering, almost magical vision in her mind of the ultimate moment of her design. Its specific outlines settled, the trio separated. Artists and scientists set to work.

Madame Ngha took personal responsibility for having the orchids gathered; determined that they should be the most beautiful flowers on earth, she had devoted all her attention, sparing no expense, to attain this end. They were selected in the Laotian jungle by well-trained experts with whose tastes she was familiar, and chosen from among hundreds for the unparalleled splendour of their tint, the elegance of their stems, and the sinuous harmony of their petals. When she herself had confirmed they were perfect, she had them dispatched to the Javanese gardener, taking every precaution to ensure that they would lose none of their freshness.

A package containing four other orchids had been sent to Sutan along with these queens of the jungle, accompanied by different, though equally precise instructions. There was no risk of these fading, but they had to be handled even more gently than the others. Similar in appearance to the natural flowers, they were the fruit of patient collaboration between Dr. Wang, with his genius for electronics, and the artist gifted at industrial design. The efforts of both had been constantly coordinated by Madame Ngha, who, involved heart and soul in this, the masterpiece of her secret-service career, took care not to allow the least flaw in its execution. As a consequence the result was perfect: the four artificial flowers could only have been distinguished from the others by an observer already familiar with two almost imperceptible marks.

*   *   *

Alone in the silent living room, Thu appeared to have finally put aside the host of importunate thoughts that had flooded in on her, and now concentrated on completing her rigorously assigned task.

She first closed the shutters, then unwrapped the bouquet and extricated a tiny box from the bed of moss. Opening this, she removed two metallic objects and an envelope. The first were the miniature tape recorders; the envelope contained both Dr. Wang's technical directions and instructions from Madame Ngha.

Thu sat down and read the first and longest part with attention. When certain she had understood and assimilated the smallest details, she got up and prepared to carry out their orders.

She began by picking out the four special orchids with the help of the marks described by Dr. Wang, and placed them to one side. She divided the rest into two bunches, keeping one to take home later. As she did this she could hardly restrain a mischievous smile at the thought that the scientist's instructions coincided so perfectly with those of the general that she was able to perform the will of each at one and the same time. She hated to disobey. Then she made two more bouquets out of those to remain here and placed each in a vase at different corners of the room, about equidistant from the piece of furniture on which the general kept his pipes. Her smile had now vanished, but aside from a slight curl of her lip she gave every appearance of carefully performing the daily duties required of her as mistress of the house. With her customary natural grace she tenderly handled the flowers, stopping at times to breathe in their fragrance, and succeeding in arranging them expressively with a few light, instinctive touches. She took even more care than usual with this task, stepping back to judge the effect from a distance and returning to correct some detail that she felt disturbed their harmony.

Nevertheless, while seeing to the artistic side, she followed Dr. Wang's instructions to the letter and in the midst of each bouquet placed one of the special orchids, arranging it with similar devotion.

She then picked up one of the minirecorders and reread the technical instructions one last time, comparing the diagram they contained with one side of the apparatus; checking her watch, she turned a dial on the panel and pushed two buttons, one after the other as prescribed, afterwards placing the instrument in a drawer of the table, leaving it slightly ajar.

One final act remained to be performed in this bungalow, but before doing that she took off her shoes and put them outside. Returning to one of the vases and taking care not to disturb the bouquet's arrangement, she deftly pressed a slight protrusion resembling a thorn at the base of the special flower. The protrusion gave way slightly under pressure.

From this moment on Thu held her breath, and even tried to suppress her heartbeat; quiet as a mouse, she walked over to the other bouquet and repeated the same operation.

Her task here was finished. After a last glance over the scene, she switched off the light and discreetly closed the door, turning the key in the lock and leaving with the remainder of the flowers and equipment.

Her own bungalow was situated about two hundred yards on the other side of the monitoring room, in a direct line with the general's lodgings. Madame Ngha had long ago been struck by this arrangement and Dr. Wang had put it to good scientific use. If anyone had seen her pass, arms filled with flowers, she would simply have been following the general's orders. This thought inspired another half-smile. Arriving home, her face still alight at this mischievous idea, she silently hurried into the living room.

'Thi Hai!'

'Yes, Madame?'

'Look at the present I received tonight.'

'Oh! Orchids, Madame! They're so rare these days.'

'They're wonderful, aren't they? I've never seen such beautiful ones before.'

'Give them to me, Madame. I'll go and put them in some water.'

'No, Thi Hai. They're a personal gift. I have to take care of them myself, or they'll bring me bad luck. You take the evening off. I won't be going out again, and I can look after John and little Thu myself. Have they been good?'

'Very good, Madame!'

'Then I'll put the orchids in their room as a reward. You can go now, I don't need you any longer.'

'Madame doesn't want me to serve dinner? The boy's already gone.'

'No. I don't need anything, and anyway, I'd rather be alone. Good night, Thi Hai.'

'Good night, Madame.'

Thu held the front door open for a second to let the phantom out, then crept into the bedroom on tiptoe. She approached the bed and, lifting the mosquito net, stood for a moment contemplating the emptiness.

'They're already asleep,' she murmured in a low voice. 'So much the better, it will be a surprise for them tomorrow morning.'

She let the net fall gently and carried out the second part of her mission here in her own room, arranging and dividing the flowers with exactly the same care and taste as she had at the general's, only breaking off now and then to glance anxiously at the bed and, with a smile, put a finger to her lips each time she heard a sigh.

Having placed the bouquets on either side of the bed, she stepped back to judge the whole effect as she had done before. Then a sudden thought seemed to strike her, and after pondering for a moment, she walked over to a little table in a far corner of the room, on which stood several photographs yellowed by age and the long stay in the jungle when Thu had been in the commandos. She had always kept them with her. There were photos of her parents and brothers and another showing her, little Thu, with John and the English couple in the forest of the high country. She had put them in her room on her arrival in Thailand, but only rarely stopped to look at them. At most she would give them a hasty glance when she came in, a distraught and furtive glance that at once revived her pained expression and made her turn to converse with her phantoms, who were so much more alive.

After a moment's hesitation she grasped these faded souvenirs in her trembling hands and placed them reverently on the night table between the two bouquets of flowers. She stepped back again, then returned to correct a few details. When she had finished, the special orchids extended their iridescent petals towards the head of the bed, like two ears bending forward to receive the murmur of tender confidences.

She decided nothing could be added to the arrangement. The only task left was to position the tape recorder at the foot of the night table, adjust it, and press the switch activating the ears of the jungle. Before performing this last act, however, she thought she heard a deep sigh from beneath the mosquito net, and raised it. She had not been mistaken. Little Thu's eyes were wide open, gazing up at her. She smiled and placed a finger to her lips.

'Go to sleep, darling,' she said in a low voice, 'You mustn't wake up John. And whatever you do, you mustn't make a sound. Now don't say a word. . . . You can look at the beautiful flowers I brought you. John will have a surprise in the morning.'

And as if sensing an unspoken question on the face of the little girl, who had leaned over towards the tape recorder, she added: 'Yes, my darling, you guessed. It's a new game, a game for children as well as grownups. Tomorrow we'll all play it together.'

Then lightly touching her lips to the child's forehead for the last time, she whispered in her ear: 'The flowers are a present from our dear Aunt Ngha and your uncle the general. You'll have to thank them.'

She withdrew on tiptoe and closed the door. With the children asleep and Thi Hai dismissed, she felt herself terribly alone in the silent living room, and her face was momentarily contorted by the fitful grimace. She quickly recovered though and, picking up the instructions included with the message, reread the second section. This was the part drafted by Madame Ngha, and it concerned her personal safety and escape. The Javanese gardener would wait for her some distance from the centre with a car and a reliable driver, who would take them as far as the Mekong. There they were to cross the river in a sampan and disembark in Laos, where agents would undertake to convey them to Vietnam. Madame Ngha ended by wishing her luck and expressed joy at the thought of seeing her dear little sister again soon.

Thu put down the piece of paper and for one last time stood pensive, suddenly gripped by the horror of her solitude. Tomorrow she would be separated from her phantoms; she knew she would never see them again. She lowered her head, her face once again disfigured by the grimace, and the heavy tear of a child overwhelmed by destiny ran down her cheek. She remained this way for a long time, prostrate, lost in a whirlwind of contradictory feelings. When she finally straightened up, her face showed greater resolution. She wiped her eyes, now gleaming strangely, and prepared to go out.

But before leaving the bungalow she granted herself one last indulgence. Opening the bedroom door slightly, without entering she blew a final kiss from her fingertips towards the bed, which now seemed bathed in a supernatural light emanating from the magic flowers. She carried this vision with her into the night.

5

General Bishop called in his adjutant to clear up various matters concerned with his departure and the closing down of the department. He did it calmly and coolly, without for a moment letting Shaw suspect that the decision taken higher up was a terrible humiliation for him. He drafted several memos to the staff, in accordance with orders received from High Command. Some of the technicians were to stay for a while under Shaw's command, to dismantle the equipment and ship it to South Vietnam, where a similar service was to be set up on a new basis under a new chief. The general was to leave the centre the day after next.

'I think everything is in order now, Shaw. Do you have anything to add?'

'Only that,' stammered the colonel, 'we are going to miss the centre in Thailand.'

'So will I.'

'And we'll miss you too, sir. All of us.'

'Thank you,' the general replied gravely. 'Now if you would leave me alone—I still have to see to my personal papers. The night promises to be calm, and I intend to take advantage of it ... although I wouldn't count on it if I were you. This last night, Shaw, I want each man at his post with as much faith and dedication as if we were installing ourselves here for a hundred years.'

'I promise, sir.'

'Good. Thu hasn't arrived yet?'

'I haven't seen her.'

'I'll need her to type all this up. But there's plenty of time. I told her myself not to hurry since ...'

Before he could finish his sentence there was a discreet knock at the door and Thu's fragile figure appeared on the threshold. She was dressed in her uniform, its only bright note still the white ribbon that always evoked the same tender emotion in the old general.

'What's the matter, Thu? You're tired, I can see that. You've been up too late recently. I'm going to find you a post where there's no more of this night duty.'

The moment she arrived she had gone to her table and begun typing one of the memos. Though she usually worked in an efficient and orderly manner, tonight she seemed unable to concentrate on even this simple task. She frequently hesitated on the keys, making mistakes and having to go back, sometimes tearing the paper out nervously and replacing it with another, only to begin the page again. Yet what had mainly motivated the general's remark was the fact that she would stop every minute or so to look at her watch, as if the time were of great importance to her that night.

'I'm all right, sir, really I am.'

'Just finish this one. It's the most urgent—then go to bed. You can type the rest tomorrow. It's late. Five minutes to eleven.'

'Five to eleven!'

There was a note of desperation in her voice. It was unlike her to pay attention to the time like this. Genuinely concerned about her, the general opened his mouth to say something, then shrugged his shoulders and turned around to empty out a drawer. After a moment Thu stopped typing altogether and sat rigidly, her fingers outstretched on the keyboard and her eyes transfixed on a nightmarish vision that revived the unbearable memories of her childhood. Astonished at the silence, the general turned back around and caught her like this, her eyes dilated as if under the effects of a drug.

'Really, Thu, there's something wrong. You should ...'

Thu's fingers mechanically started typing again. The general stopped, hesitated, then decided to go back to his work. He did not have the curiosity to go and see what was happening on the memo. If he had, he would have found that the keys were typing out not a single word of his text, and much of the time not even words, but only a meaningless series of letters. With certain exceptions, however: while Thu's features contorted intensely and she muttered imperceptibly with trembling lips, her fingers unconsciously composed and repeated the word 'massacre', the only significant refrain in this preposterous litany.

Eleven o'clock. The general had begun tearing up papers and throwing them into the wastebasket when Colonel Shaw burst into the office. Thu stared at him and her fingers again froze on the keyboard.

'Engine noises, sir, following one another rapidly. Trucks and half-tracks. No doubt a large convoy. Four sensors are reporting it.'

'Connect the speakers.'

The general's voice shook despite his efforts to appear calm. Not yet daring to thank God for his miraculous answer to his prayers, he listened with a tremor of hope to the roar of engines now reverberating through his office.

He pushed a first button. The relevant area appeared on the illuminated screen. Two red dots flickered, barely distinguishable from each other. The ears of the jungle could only have been a few yards apart on the ground. But it was enough to permit the IBM to indicate the outline of a convoy with a dotted blue line.

'A new route,' remarked the general. 'I don't know that area. It's the first time we've had signals from there.'

Colonel Shaw was perfectly indifferent to the location, but he looked worried: the dotted line signified the computer had insufficient data to define the convoy exactly. Thu stood up and approached the screen. She too seemed anxious for some further information. It was not long in coming.

'Look, sir, another ear.'

'Two,' Shaw corrected her. 'They're very close together.'

Two more red lights had just appeared, situated a few hundred yards from the preceding ones and, like them, almost indistinguishable. Shaw let out a cheer. The IBM had received more data, and the blue serpent of the convoy promptly grew into a fairly long continuous line making its way along the path defined by the ears of the jungle, its 'head' now almost level with the first dots.

'An extremely important convoy,' bellowed the general. 'I'll call for a zero alert. That will mobilize all available F-4's.'

He pressed the button provided for this type of operation, then finally the last one, which connected the IBM S 360/65 with the computers aboard the aircraft.

'Now all we have to do is wait,' he muttered, managing to regain an appearance of composure, though only at the cost of an effort that made the veins on his forehead bulge.

6

Air Force Lieutenant Jim Douglas was flying over Vietnam. At his altitude the air was clear, and he had no difficulty spotting the other planes. Visibility towards the ground, however, was nil: a thick layer of low cloud covered the jungle. As was the rule in such cases, navigation and bomb-release lay entirely in the hands of the computers. The pilots themselves took no part in the operation.

In the darkness, with nothing to hold his attention, Lieutenant Douglas was overcome by a rather bad case of the blues, and felt at such a loss that for no real reason he put his mouth to the microphone and called his flight leader.

'Do you know where we're going, sir?'

'Haven't the faintest idea, Jim. Some place that's going to get it, that's all I know. For the moment we're headed north-west. Probably Laos. But it's been a long time since I worried about that sort of thing. What's got into you, anyway, asking such ridiculous questions?'

'Bored, sir,' moaned Douglas plaintively.

'Bored? Why don't you try what I'm doing?'

'What's that sir?'

'Reading a detective story. Just hope I can finish this chapter before we start bombing. After that all I have to do is report back to base, mission accomplished, and they'll take over for our return flight. Hope I can get another chapter in before we land.'

'But I don't have any detective stories, sir.'

'Better think about that next time.'

'But the trouble is, sir . . .'

'What now, Jim?'

'The trouble is, we never meet any enemy aircraft. It just dawned on me. . . .'

'I'm beginning to get irritated, Jim. This is no time to start carrying on—we're on a mission!'

'Are you sure there's no chance of running into the enemy some night?'

'I'm as sure of it as you're talking crap. I suppose that's really going to upset you, isn't it? Aren't the SAMs and AA enough?'

'There's not even that tonight,' Douglas grumbled again. 'Sir . . .'

'Listen, Jim, why don't you think about something cheerful—like the end of the war, or getting back home. And if that doesn't work, count to a hundred. If you do it slow enough, it'll probably get you to the target. But in the meantime, lay off. I've still got two more pages to go. Night, Jim.'

Jim Douglas heaved a sigh and tried to follow his superior's advice.

* * *

'That's odd,' remarked General Bishop, looking thoughtfully at the illuminated screen where several ears of the jungle were flickering. 'That's odd, there's something about this region that brings back memories, but I can't pin-point it.'

Thu hastily cut in.

'I think I recognize it, sir ... it's a valley near the Laotian frontier, but I can't remember the name. I think the map's defective.... Our maps are often inaccurate, we've already discovered that, sir.... Take this river for instance...'

She stood up and started talking volubly, saying anything to distract his attention. She grabbed a ruler and on the large map of Indochina that hung on the wall opposite the screen, showing the gaps made by the defoliants in red, pointed at random to a spot near Laos.

'It's here, I'm sure. But the river doesn't cross the trail like the map on the screen indicates. Look, sir. On the contrary, it runs parallel to it for quite a way.'

'It's insane,' said the general furiously. 'I'm going to protest to Headquarters about these maps.... Anyway, the F-4's can't be far from their objective.'

Colonel Shaw had taken out his watch and was frowning.

'Sir, if it's the point Thu indicated, they should have dropped their bombs two minutes ago.'

In an instant he had calculated the distance between this point and the F-4 base and, having all the relevant data in his head—transmission delay, takeoff time, speed of the aircraft—knew to the exact second when the bombing should occur.

'There's never been such a large discrepancy before,' he insisted. 'You must be mistaken, Thu. It's not there; it's much farther from their base.'

Having said that, he immediately reacted as anyone else would have and went towards the screen to locate the point's position. General Bishop, though somewhat slower had exactly the same impulse.

'It's simple enough to check, Shaw. You look at the co-ordinates on the screen and I'll verify them on the map.'

Again Thu wanted to intervene, but words failed her. She couldn't think of anything that would divert them. Shaw leaned over the screen and read out:

'Longitude: one hundred four degrees seventeen minutes; latitude: sixteen degrees thirty-three minutes, sir.'

'One hundred four degrees seventeen minutes; sixteen degrees thirty-three minutes,' repeated the general. 'Let's see.... No, let me, Thu. It'll do me good to get a little exercise.'

He had hoisted himself up on the little stool Thu used to keep the huge map up to date and, rejecting the offer of the young girl as she hastened to take his place, laboriously traced the parallels of latitude and longitude with his finger.

'One hundred four degrees seventeen minutes, sixteen degrees thirty-three minutes,' he repeated again. 'Thu, you made a mistake. Shaw was right. It's much farther west.'

'I told you,' said the colonel with satisfaction.

'Farther west and a little farther north ...'

His finger continued to painstakingly follow the lines. Standing now on tiptoe, he leaned to his left until he was almost off balance.

'It's ... Oh!'

He let out a gasp, was silent for a moment, then burst into a tremendous laugh that shook his whole body, to such an extent that Thu and Shaw had to help him down from his perch.

'What is it, sir?' asked the colonel, worried.

'That beats everything!' stammered General Bishop.

The ludicrous discovery he had just made, added to the tension of the past few days, brought on a hysterical fit of laughter that kept him from saying anything at all. It took him a full minute to regain his composure.

'You'll never guess, Shaw: one hundred four degrees seventeen minutes, sixteen degrees thirty-three minutes is not in Vietnam, not even in Laos—it's in Thailand.'

'In Thailand!'

'Better than that, Shaw, much better than that. These are—are you ready?—these are the exact coordinates of our base. I'm such an idiot—they completely skipped my mind. Huh, Thu?'

Thu echoed the general's laughter as boisterously as she could. But Shaw didn't share their hilarity.

'Good God,' he cried out, again leaning over the illuminated screen where the long blue serpent representing the convoy continued its slow progress and was now almost between the two scintillating red dots. 'Good God, it's true. This river—it's ours!'

'And this large rectangle, it's the landing field for the B-52's. There's no doubt about it, my friend: your computer's mixed up the cards. You won't be able to pretend it's infallible after this.'

'But you don't understand the situation!' yelled the maddened colonel. 'The IBM S 360/65 is never wrong, sir.'

General Bishop suddenly stopped laughing.

'Never, Shaw, never—you're absolutely sure?'

'Absolutely, sir. Never.'

'But then ... ?'

His brain made the same effort as his adjutant's, though somewhat belatedly.

'But then that means the F-4's are obeying ... and at this very moment heading ...'

'No doubt about it, sir.'

The general rushed to his desk, where a special phone kept him in direct contact with General Headquarters. It was out of order. Taking advantage of his agitation, Thu had torn out the wire a moment before.

'Shaw, go call ...'

At the same instant Shaw rushed out of the room bombs started hitting the centre. The monitoring room's sound-proofing had muffled the noise of the plane's engines right up to the last moment. The first explosions were heard live and at the same time indirectly over the loud-speakers via the orchids of the jungle.

Everything went dead: the blue serpent, the red dots on the screen, the screen itself. The equipment ceased transmission as all hell broke loose over the centre, pulverizing the bungalows and monitoring service and hammering the B-52 base. Every last bit of precious equipment was completely destroyed, the IBM S 360/65 transformed into shapeless debris and fine ash. Every member of the staff perished at his post. Thu and General Bishop were among the first struck down by a direct hit. She had instinctively taken refuge beside him, as if seeking protection there.

7

'Sutan has just arrived,' said Van. 'Everything went as planned. Except that he's alone.'

'Thu's not with him?'

'He's alone,' repeated Van, shaking her head sadly.

'Tell him to come in.'

The Javanese gardener entered the office and, removing his cap, greeted her respectfully but with an ease that showed long-standing membership in the service. His features were drawn. He looked tired, hardly having slept since his departure from Thailand and the journey across Laos. Madame Ngha, who could speak all the languages of South-east Asia, questioned him in his own Malay.

'A success, Mem,' he replied to her first question, instinctively giving her the title the Malays once gave European women. 'The planes arrived on schedule. Judging from the noise, there were a large number. The bombing was terrible.'

'I know. Our enemies themselves have not been able to

hide their losses. The entire world has become informed. It's a great psychological victory for us.'

'I was waiting a few miles from the base, where it was arranged I would meet Thu.'

'Thu? Tell me what happened to her.'

'Thu didn't come. She should have been there well before the bombing, since that was the prearranged signal for our flight. There was plenty of time, and she couldn't have been mistaken about the meeting place. She knew that crossroads very well. Thu didn't come; I just don't understand.'

A shadow crossed Madame Ngha's brow. But she motioned the Javanese to go on with his story.

'Did you wait?'

'For a long time. I stayed through the whole raid. A stray bomb even fell near our car. I heard the planes and suddenly saw the sky over the base on fire. The B-52 fuel depot was in flames. I climbed a tree, and the hangars, the planes, the monitoring centre, the bungalows, everything was ablaze. They aimed well.'

'Our enemies always aim well,' said Madame Ngha.

'And Thu still didn't come. I waited, long, long after the bombing, contrary to instructions. The driver wanted to go. We had a fight and I had to threaten him with my knife. They were very trying hours, Mem. I wondered if maybe she had been caught preparing the trap.'

'It certainly wasn't that, otherwise it wouldn't have worked.'

'Yes, it was stupid of me, and that's what I ended up saying to myself. But I didn't know what else to think.'

'As always, she performed her mission perfectly. We should be grateful to her ... and to you as well. This is the finest achievement of our war. I know a great many B-52's were destroyed, besides the monitoring centre. I'll see to it you are congratulated and receive a fitting reward.'

'If it's one of the most famous achievements of the war, as Mem says, then it's the brain behind it that should be congratulated.'

From the highest to the lowest levels of the hierarchy,

those who had participated in the operation and so knew it at least in outline, if not in detail, were lost in admiration for the genius capable of conceiving such a brilliant manoeuvre. They were not very far from considering Madame Ngha a magician. She now gave an imperceptible smile and lowered her head slightly: she could be sensitive to flattery on occasion, if it was well put, and especially if its object was the power and subtlety of her mind. Another shadow then darkened her brow.

'So, Thu didn't come.'

'Thu didn't come,' repeated the Javanese despondently. 'I waited most of the night. I only decided to flee when I was sure there was no longer any hope. The driver took me as far as the Mekong. The rest of the way was easy. But I still don't know how to feel about it. I liked Thu very much, Mem.'

'Yes, well, don't think about it any more. That's what I'm going to try and do. You take fifteen days' leave, and I'll see you again afterward.'

The gardener saluted and turned on his heels. Near the door he finally plucked up the courage to ask a question.

'I liked Thu very much,' he repeated humbly, 'like everyone who knew her. Does Mem, who has eyes and ears everywhere, even among our enemies, think she could have escaped some other way, and that we might see her again one day?'

'I don't think so,' said Madame Ngha.

For a long time after the gardener had left she remained silent and sombre. Then, with a sudden gesture, as if chasing away an unwelcome idea, she abruptly changed the subject. Van knew she was grappling with a disturbing problem.

'We must send the map of the Ho Chi Minh Way to Minister Kim,' she said. 'It's of no more use to us. We won't be able to add anything to it now, and he'll need it for his projects.'

Van assured her she would, but couldn't resist coming

back to the subject she felt was tormenting both of them.

'I also liked Thu very much.'

'You didn't know her,' said Madame Ngha aggressively.

'I never met her, but I've read her reports.'

'So? ... and I,' she said almost violently, 'you think I didn't love her?'

'What do you think could have happened to her?' insisted Van with rare audacity.

'I doubt if any secret service will ever know,' replied Madame Ngha in the same tone, 'not even the best, not even mine.'

Van bowed her head. After a few moments, in spite of her boss's temper, she ventured another remark: 'Her last reports insisted on the polite and benevolent, even paternal, way the general treated her. There was a sense of gratitude, a certain compassion, perhaps.'

'Maybe,' said Madame Ngha distantly.

'It seemed as if she had come to regard him as a chivalrous opponent. Isn't it possible that at the last minute she might have felt a kind of ... well, remorse maybe, seeing the cruel way we were treating him, the way we were driving him to his own destruction, and finally dishonour, since he's bound to be considered responsible for the disaster.'

'This chivalrous opponent, as you call him, was the brother in arms of those who massacred her entire family. Even if you happen to have lost sight of that, do you think Thu could have forgotten?'

'That's true.'

'And he caused the death of hundreds of our people before we turned his own weapons against him.'

'That's true too ... but if I still insist, it's because of a fantasy I often had while reading over Thu's reports.'

'A fantasy, Van?' asked Madame Ngha in a peculiar tone.

'I tried to imagine what her life must have been like there.'

'You can always use your imagination. But the main thing

is not to let yourself be imprisoned by it.... What did you imagine?'

'That maybe, on that base in Thailand, a country she described as peaceful, far from the war and its horrors, and in an atmosphere the general did his best to make congenial, she had succeeded in rediscovering a little of the serenity unknown to her since childhood. So the idea of losing this comparative peace might have seemed intolerable to her, and ...'

Intimidated by Madame Ngha's stare, however, she did not finish her sentence. Yet her boss seemed neither surprised nor shocked.

'I told you no secret service will ever know the truth. One can only dream, as you said, and your dreams are worth as much as mine. But it's a possibility I've considered too.'

'Then do you think ... ?'

'I'm not thinking, I'm dreaming. Thu was a girl from Hue, Van, and the girls of Hue are different from those in the north and south. I thought I knew her well, but one never knows what might be going on in their minds.'

There was now a note of compassion in her voice, and Van thought she could detect in it a strong emotion. But, except for brief moments, Madame Ngha forbade herself this kind of indulgence, and she continued coolly: 'But it's a possibility I've rejected.'

'And so ... ?'

'I prefer to believe she was prompted to stay by a keen sense of duty.'

'Of duty?'

'Try to think, Van, as I am, instead of dreaming. It's almost always more advisable. Despite our precautions, there was a good chance the deception would be discovered, even at the final stage. For example, someone could have heard the tape recordings. There was a risk too that the general or one of his assistants might have noticed in time that the monitoring centre was the target.... And also, Van, Thu's very absence might have aroused suspicion. Wouldn't it then have been natural to send someone over to her bungalow to see what she was doing? ... Someone who might well have discovered the trap? She must have turned all this over in her mind, weighing the pros and cons ... and being a first-class agent, like all those I select, she was prepared to make any sacrifice to ensure the success of her mission. Don't you agree?'

Van did not reply. Madame Ngha continued with increasing vehemence, as if trying to convince herself.

'She correctly judged that her role, as I had outlined it, was unfinished. During her training here I had told her that a good agent must always show initiative and at times even disobey orders. She believed she could best fulfill this role by staying, and maybe gain us precious minutes by diverting the authorities' attention. It's not the first time one of us has taken a sense of duty to the point of sacrificing himself, if the end seemed worth it. And it was worth it.'

'A rare act of heroism. And Thu was capable of it. All the same, maybe ...'

'You irritate me with your maybes,' Madame Ngha suddenly broke in with blunt impatience. 'I know what you're going to say, that maybe there were several motives behind her strange conduct? Maybe a charitable Providence created some miraculous correspondence between her duty and her hopeless nostalgia? Maybe we two are crazy to search for reasons. Maybe she didn't think at all. Maybe her body, weary and full of loathing, was completely detached from her mind and obeyed its own irresistible impulse. Maybe ... maybe we must see in her senseless behaviour the insane issue of one of those strange situations sometimes born out of the confluence of two separate worlds, our own and the West, with the war acting as a catalyst, or rather as a fertile dung heap that breeds and nourishes to absurd proportions the monstrous flowers of extravagance. In any case ...'

Little by little she had worked herself into a state of frenzy her secretary had never seen in her before. But then, pausing, she took two or three deep breaths, as if to rid herself of an intolerable weight, and returned to the measured tone more appropriate to her position.

'In any case, Van, we must keep to the theory of sacrifice. That's certainly the one I shall present to our people, and it is her heroism that will be praised in the citation I'll request for her. I want to make this absolutely clear so that you don't indulge in mindless prattle and suggest anything else.'

'I understand, Madame,' said her secretary, nodding.

'Very good ... and don't forget to have that map sent to Minister Kim.'

Van went towards the wall, climbed on the stool, and took the map off its nail. She turned around to face her boss and began to roll the chart up slowly, stopping at each turn, taking infinite care not to crease it. Silently, Madame Ngha watched this operation to the end, her face slightly drawn, though in her eyes whose depths shone with the fierce gleam that had earned her her flattering nickname, still lingered a vision of the scarlet furrow that crossed the map from North to South: the bloody gash of the Ho Chi Minh Way.